Outer Banks
Mysteries &
Seaside
Stories

CHARLES H. WHEDBEE

Outer Banks Mysteries & Seaside Stories

JOHN F. BLAIR, *Publisher*

Winston-Salem, North Carolina

Copyright © 1978 by Charles H. Whedbee
Library of Congress Catalog Card Number: 78–58535
ISBN 0–89587–006–1
Printed in the United States of America

Seventh Printing, 1991

Library of Congress Cataloging in Publication Data

Whedbee, Charles Harry.
    Outer Banks Mysteries and Seaside Stories.

    1.   Outer Banks, N.C.—History—Miscellanea.
2. Folk-lore—North Carolina—Outer Banks. 3. Legends—
North Carolina—Outer Banks. I. Title.
F262.096W47   975.6′1   78–58535
ISBN 0–89587–006–1

For Sallie L. & Harry W. Whedbee

Contents

Foreword

"What happens twice will happen three times."
This is a saying that has been prevalent on the Outer Banks of North Carolina for many generations. Many people believe it and can cite you example after convincing example of its truth.

Certainly it is true in the case of this little volume, the third in a series dealing with the folk tales and legends of that fabulous region which played such an important part in the beginnings of our country. The other two books have received kind reception and generous acceptance. It is hoped that this effort will likewise be pleasing to the folklore buffs as well as to the folks who just love a good tale.

Not all these tales are set on or by the sea. Some of them are said to have taken place on the broad sounds and rivers that were the highways of our early settlers. All of them have the salty scent of coastal Carolina, and they are genuine parts of our history as a colony and then as a state. All are true to the times and places in which they are said to have occurred.

Charles Harry Whedbee

Whalebone Junction
Nag's Head, North Carolina

Outer Banks
Mysteries &
Seaside
Stories

I

The Indian Gallows

THE AMERICAN LIVE oak, one of the most beautiful evergreens, is entwined in the history and legend of the Carolina coastland. Sturdy and majestic, it is said to grow one hundred years, live one hundred years, and die one hundred years. Be that as it may, there are many ancient specimens still beautifying the landscape, and one of them, located in the deep woods of Colington Island, just west of the Wright Brothers Monument, is the locale of one of the most persistent and touching legends of this storied region.

This tree is called the "Indian Gallows Tree," and it was one of two live oaks growing within ten feet of each other. In time, a large limb from one of the trees grew out in the direction of the other tree, and the tip of that limb actually pierced and grew into the trunk of its neighbor, until the entire joinder developed into a huge letter H with the cross-bar, or cross-limb, being a good ten feet off the ground. This cross-limb put out shoots from the top, giving the whole thing the appearance of a garlanded archway, with the top of the arch being almost perfectly level and parallel with the surface of the ground beneath. Thus the trees grew long before our land was formed into a nation, and thus they continued until the early years of the present century, when one of the majestic trees died and was cut and carved into small souvenirs by the people who visited the place and were fascinated by the story connected with it.

According to our legend, in 1711 the family of Robert Austin was cast ashore in a shipwreck on the Outer Banks of what was to become North Carolina. Luckier than most, the Austins were able to salvage many of their worldly goods with the help of a friendly hunting party of Tuscarora Indians. Their lives and their property safe, the survivors began looking for a place to settle and begin the process of carving their homestead out of the lush wilderness.

Here again the Indians were a great deal of assistance, transporting the new settlers in their canoes and pointing out likely locations.

Foremost among these newfound friends was the handsome son of the chief of the tribe, a young brave called Prince Roanoke. One of the chief attractions of the English family, at least in the eyes of Roanoke, was the Austin's beautiful daughter Elnora, a typical English beauty with deep blue eyes, a peaches-and-cream complexion, and a wealth of long, silky blonde hair. Elnora liked the young Indian prince and valued him as a true friend in this wilderness, but that was as far as it went with her. She was betrothed to one Henry Redwine, who had promised to follow her to the New World and make her his wife just as soon as he had worked out his apprenticeship to a silversmith and was free to leave England.

Finally a suitable place for the Austins' home was found on the north end of Roanoke Island, and here they began clearing a small patch of ground, setting out net stakes in the nearby sound, and generally making ready to work a living out of the land and sea.

The weather was mild and the Indians continued to be friendly, so things began to look bright and hopeful for the little family of settlers in that good year 1711. Prince Roanoke visited the area often, and he and the young and beautiful Elnora took long walks together, communicating as best they could and dreaming the dreams of youth everywhere.

Roanoke could not conceal his love for the English maid and told her of it on one lovely moonlit night as they strolled on the peaceful, wave-lapped shore of the island. She heard him out, and, misty-eyed with empathy and understanding, she told him that her heart belonged to her English lover and that she must remain true to her vow. She was bound by her heart as well as her vow to await his coming to the New World and the establishment of their home. Heartbroken and ashamed, Roanoke returned to his home up the mighty river. Hope is the last thing that dies in a man, however, and in the months that followed he returned occasionally to visit with his kin on the island and to talk and walk again with his beloved Elnora.

If things were hopeful and bright in the Austin household, they were anything but peaceful in the heart and mind and in the dreams of old King Cashie, monarch of all the Tuscarora tribes and the father of the young Prince Roanoke. King Cashie hated the intruding whites with all his savage heart, and he never ceased to dream of the day when they would be driven from his once happy and uncongested hunting and fishing grounds.

History now records that it was in the year 1712 that he secretly began to form his "Tuscarora Confederacy," a joining together of the various Tuscarora families with the Coree Indians and the Matchapunga Indians to the south and east in a common bond of mistrust of the new settlers and resentment of their presence.

Finally, in 1713 a plan for the massacre of all the whites began to take shape. There were many councils held deep in the woods, where the various chiefs discussed strategy and the chances for winning such a war of extermination.

Prince Roanoke knew about these meetings, of course. He even attended some of them. He was familiar with his father's hatred of the white men, but he never really believed anything drastic would result from all these meetings and rantings. He avoided such gatherings when he could find a good excuse.

So it befell that the young prince was as much surprised as anyone when he learned that the Tuscarora Confederacy had evolved into a Tuscarora council of war. A definite plan had been made, and dates had actually been set for a concerted attack on all white settlements and outlying farms in the region. An intricate time schedule had been adopted to coordinate the various attacks.

All was to be done by stealth, of course, and every effort was to be made to take the whites by surprise and thus make their annihilation easier. No one—man, woman, or child—was to be spared. The war was to be treated as a holy war, and all must die.

Immediately Roanoke's thoughts turned to his beloved Elnora and the certainty of her fate when the raiding band assigned to her island should arrive at her small cabin. King Cashie had planned that his son and heir-apparent should take a leading part in the execution of these massacres, but the young brave had quite different intentions.

Slipping quietly away at midnight from his father's village up the mighty Chowan River, the young prince crept silently to where he had hidden his small, fast canoe. He shoved it off from the shore, sprang in, and moved out onto the broad bosom of the river. Heading downstream as rapidly as his paddle could drive him, he hurried toward the island where his beloved slept, quite unmindful of her grave danger.

On and on glided the small boat, with Roanoke trying to conserve his strength and yet gain as much distance as possible before the growing light of dawn forced him to hide on shore. There he rested and slept until the falling darkness sent him once again on his errand of mercy.

Arriving at long last at the island where he had left his beloved, he was startled and dismayed to see tall flames leaping skyward from the direction of the Austin homestead. Hiding his canoe in the tall marsh grass at the north end of the island, the young prince crept stealthily through the woods until he came near the clearing he knew so well. The scene that he had feared to find lay before his eyes. The Austin home and all the outbuildings were aflame, and there in the farmyard, gun in hand, lay the lifeless body of Robert Austin, the shaft of an arrow protruding from between his shoulder blades.

A few feet away lay the body of Mrs. Austin, one arm extended toward her husband as if in a final effort to help him before the crushing, mangling blow of the tomahawk had ended her dream of the good life in this new world. Neither body had been scalped. The Indians had not yet learned this grisly trick from renegade white men.

Elnora was not to be seen anywhere, nor were any of the raiding party in evidence. Unwilling to venture into the clearing from the comparative safety of the forest, Roanoke lay perfectly motionless and silent until the fires burned themselves out and darkness once again enveloped the scene. Still there was no trace of Elnora or of the raiding Indians.

One last chance remained. A little to the south of the northernmost tip of the island there was a hidden cave right at the water's edge where storm tides had carved out a large hole under the overhanging bank. Roanoke and Elnora had walked there many times during their visits together and, as far as he knew, only the two of them were aware of the cave's existence.

With downcast heart and faint hope, the young brave threaded his way through the underbrush until he came to the hidden mouth of the cave. It was pitch black inside and completely silent, but he dared not make a light. With a sigh of despair, he was turning away from the hiding place when he heard a sob, a very human sob, from that dark hole. Rushing to the very end of the cave, he found his Elnora safe and sound but almost hysterical with grief and fear.

Clasping her tightly in his arms, he rocked slowly back and forth and made little comforting noises until she became calmer. Finally she was able to sob out the account of how she had been at the edge of the clearing when she saw the raiding party of painted Indians descend on her homestead, kill her mother and father, and set fire to the buildings. In their frenzy and war lust, the Indians had not even seen Elnora in the darkness, and she had run blindly, not even knowing the way she ran, until she found herself at the cave. There she had hidden in mortal terror until the young prince had arrived.

Now the young couple was faced with the even greater danger of trying to avoid the raiding Indian war parties who were ravaging the isolated white settlements of the Albemarle. Their only hope lay in reaching Edenton, far up the broad reaches of the Albemarle Sound and the Chowan River. They now knew that capture would mean their torture and death by the traditional Indian method, being burned alive while strapped to a sturdy post or stake. Daylight travel was out of the question. Their sole chance lay in traveling at night and hiding by day.

This is exactly what they did. Their first night of travel was made more secure, if much more difficult, by the arising of a great storm. Strong winds and driving rain hid them from spying eyes but also nearly swamped the little canoe and made it much more difficult to handle. Fortunately they had a following wind that drove the small craft before it like a chip on the ocean, sometimes almost driving it under the waves, but at other times causing it to plane over the following sea. All that stormy night the young Roanoke paddled and steered his canoe toward the

Chowan while Elnora tried desperately to bail the boat with her cupped hands. It was a wild night.

As the cold, gray first light of approaching dawn spread across the eastern sky behind them, they beached their boat on a sand spit that projected from the shore. They disembarked and dragged the canoe up into the shelter of a dense pine forest. Roanoke then went back and, with a branch broken from a pine tree, carefully walked backward as he wiped from the sand the keel mark of the little boat and the footprints of the travelers. When he returned to the hiding place in the trees, even the most careful searcher would have been unable to tell that anyone or anything had passed that way.

Completely spent, the two young fugitives lay down on the forest floor and, cushioned by a centuries-old carpet of pine needles, dropped quickly into the deep sleep of exhaustion. Food was not a problem. They would have been too bone-weary to eat, even if they had had food. During the morning the wind subsided into a gentle southerly breeze, and the rain continued to fall steadily, hissing through the needles of the pine trees and dropping softly to the ground.

At sunset Roanoke awoke, and while Elnora slept, he carefully scouted the area. He found nothing to increase his apprehension, but he did discover some berries and some edible pine tree buds, which he carefully gathered just as long as he could see in the fading light. Returning to the canoe, he found Elnora awake and anxious to continue their journey. After eating their meager meal, the two climbed back into the canoe and resumed their flight toward what they hoped would be safety.

It was an hour before daybreak when the headland of Edenton loomed before them. They reached the town wharf just as the townfolk and fishermen were beginning to come out of their houses to begin another day's work.

Excitement and indignation buzzed through the little town as the story of the massacre and the flight of the survivors spread like wildfire. Well did they know, these pioneers in this lush wilderness, that vengeful old King Cashie would not delay long in trying to apprehend any fugitives from his raids and to wipe out the settlement on the banks of the Chowan. Attack, they knew, was imminent.

Riding at anchor in the wide harbor of Edenton, there lay a fat merchant ship that had arrived only hours before with a cargo of, among other things, powder and shot and several dozen muskets. It may well have been the passage of that very ship up the waters of the sound which so frightened the raiding Indians that they did not try to pursue Roanoke and Elnora in their frail canoes, if indeed they had any knowledge of the couple's desperate flight.

Wonder of wonders, at least for Elnora, not only did the ship contain supplies and weapons, but it also held the person of her beloved Henry Redwine, free from his apprenticeship and come to claim his bride and his future in the New World. For Henry and Elnora, happiness was complete. Their sorrow at the death of her parents was softened by the joy of their reunion.

Not so, however, for Roanoke. He now saw his last chance of winning the beautiful English girl fade away to nothing. He was also faced with what he knew would be the anger and malice of his own father, King Cashie. He was, indeed, a man without a family, without a hope for the future.

In Edenton, history tells us, preparations for defense went forward rapidly. Log walls were erected just outside the town and redoubts of earth were thrown up to give shelter to the defenders. There were those in the community who looked askance at the presence of the young Prince Roanoke in their midst as all this was going on. But he worked so willingly along with the settlers in the preparation of the defenses, even scouting the nearby forests daily for signs of approaching Indians, that the people began to accept him as their true ally. One by one, the murmurings against him ceased.

When the attack finally did come, it was fierce but short-lived. The settlers were too well organized, and their musket fire from behind both log and earthen walls was too devastating for the Indians to bear. They fell back, carrying their dead and wounded with them. What finally broke the spirit of the attackers was a well-placed cannonball from one of the deck guns of the armed merchant ship. The ball landed right in the midst of a group of Indians, killing several and breaking the leg of King Cashie himself.

They fell back in disarray and never again seriously threatened Edenton, which continued to be too well armed and disciplined for the forces the Indians could muster thereafter. Although raids on isolated farms continued, the uprising of the Tuscarora Confederacy had just about run its course.

There now began for the young Prince Roanoke a most frustrating and sorrowful time. He could not safely return to his own people, and yet he felt very much an outcast in the town of Edenton. Forgetting how well he had served them in the recent armed conflict, many of the whites distrusted him just because he was an Indian.

Elnora and her new husband were consistently kind and thoughtful toward the young brave and did their best to relieve his loneliness, but to little avail. Their very kindness served to deepen the pain of seeing his beloved happily married to another man.

Finally Roanoke decided to take the fateful step that would either solve many of his problems or else end them once and for all. He would return, an eighteenth century prodigal son, to his father's tribe. He labored under no illusions about the cruelty of Indian justice. He knew his father's temperament, but after all, he was the only son of the old chief, and he believed that, in his own savage way, the old man loved him.

Days and weeks went by as the young prince prepared himself for his journey of homecoming. He searched the woods with persistence until he found just the perfect specimen of turkey-cock to yield the golden-bronze feathers for his girdle and a splendid white heron to furnish the head decoration to which he was entitled by tribal law in recognition of his accomplishments as a youth. Prime quality doeskin for his cape and tanned otter furs for his loincloth were available from local trappers and hunters. Finally his ceremonial costume was complete and perfect according to Indian tribal protocol.

Roanoke looked every inch the chief as he stood on the wooded edge of Oakum Street in Edenton and bade good-bye to his white friends. Tears filled the eyes of the young brave and the newlyweds as they shook hands with friendly palms cupped on each other's shoulders. Finally, with a tremendous heave of his young shoulders, Roanoke turned away from his friends, walked to where his frail canoe floated, and paddled off eastward over the broad bosom of Albemarle Sound.

It seems almost certain that the young prince was shadowed from the very start and for almost the entire journey down the sound. At any rate, when he finally reached his father's village, a committee of young braves was waiting for him. He was roughly seized, carried into the Indian village, and forthwith tied to a man-high stake set deeply into the sand.

There he remained, without food or drink, until nightfall, when the neighboring chiefs began to arrive to convene the court that would decide his fate. Throughout all that day and during the entire night-long trial that followed, Prince Roanoke uttered never a word. He did not seek to defend himself or to offer excuses or reasons as subchief after subchief made long, emotional speeches accusing him of traitorous conduct, of being responsible for the failure of their holy war, and of being entirely false and untrue to his father, his tribe, and the Tuscarora Confederacy. One after another, they all demanded that he be put to death for his sins against his people. Some of the orators even went so far as to spit in his face and strike him with their ceremonial gourds. King Cashie uttered not one word in defense of his son.

Finally the vote was taken, just as the day began to break over the forest. The decision of the chiefs was unanimous—death to the traitor. Because of the young brave's royal heritage, the chiefs decided to allow the old king to decide the manner of his son's execution.

Rising to his feet, with all the glory of the rising sun spreading its light behind him, the ancient and crippled king denounced Prince Roanoke and, with no show of sorrow whatsoever, disclaimed him as a son.

"He has loved the white man well," intoned the old chief, "and he has reaped the reward of the white man's fickleness. Let him, therefore, not be granted the ancient Indian execution of fire at the stake but, rather, the shameful death on the gallows by which the white thieves kill their own criminals." His voice rising to almost an hysterical scream, the vengeful old Cashie spat out, "Let the traitor be hanged by the neck until he is dead, dead, dead!"

With savage shouts of approval, the Indian braves seized the young prince again. They tore away the deerskin thongs binding him to the ceremonial post and threw them into the sand. With eager haste, they dragged him through the forest by the hair of his head, through brambles and thorns and across little creeks until they reached the giant oaks with the peculiar cross-branch between their trunks.

Hastily fashioning a noose of rope, they placed it around Roanoke's neck and threw the other end over the cross-branch. They hoisted the bound Roanoke, kicking, into the air and hung him by the neck until he was indeed "dead, dead, dead." Thus ends the legend of the Indian Gallows Tree.

As early as the year 1846, Col. William H. Rhodes of Bertie County published a poem entitled "The Indian Gallows," which concludes with the Indian trial as old King Cashie exclaims:

> No! not the stake . . . .
> He loves the pale-face; brothers, let him die
> The white man's death! come, let us bend a tree
> And swing the traitor, as the Red-men see
> The pale-faced villain hang; give not the stake
> To him who would the Red-man's freedom take
> Who from our fathers and our God would roam,
> And strives to rob us of our lands and home!
>
> * * * * *
>
> They seize him now, and drag him to the spot
> Where death awaits, and pangs are all forgot.

There are those familiar with the area who say that the legend is not ended yet. They say that sometimes, when the moon is full and the wind is still, you will hear the sound of mourning and keening and weeping, and the little creek that runs by the gallows will run red as blood.

2

The Gray Man of Hatteras

HE YEAR WAS 1966 AND it was just four days until Labor Day. The Coast Guard of Cape Hatteras was busy with one of its assigned chores, warning the summer visitors as well as the year-round residents of the approach of that year's big hurricane. It was certain that the big wind was expected to pass directly over Cape Hatteras, and the word was either to get out while there was time or else to get to a place of safety with all deliberate speed.

Already the wind was blowing a full gale, and the mist and spume from the sea rolled over the beaches as Apprentice Seaman Brooks, newly out of the boot camp at the Coast Guard Academy, led his detachment of men along the beach near Cape Point.

They had just visited the last cottage near the beach, and their work was completed. They were walking back to the spot where they had parked their beach vehicle.

Then they saw it! There, standing just in the break of

the seaward dunes, was the figure of a human wearing a sou'wester and slowly swinging his right arm as though to motion someone to come back from the beach and seek the shelter of the dunes.

All but one of the men in the party knew immediately what they were seeing. That one, an outlander recently assigned to service on the Outer Banks, ran toward the shadowy figure, shouting a warning as he ran. The figure turned and faced the runner until barely ten feet separated them. Then it vanished. It just disappeared into the air.

If it was a human, there was no place for him to have hidden. There were no footprints where he had been standing. A search of the nearby beach produced nothing, and the newcomer began to doubt his own eyesight.

When he returned to his group, they explained to the newcomer as gently as they could that what had been seen was not a human but was the familiar Gray Man of Hatteras.

Since the early nineteen hundreds the Gray Man has appeared on that stretch of beach between Cape Point and the Hatteras Lighthouse every time a hurricane threatens. He always appears to be trying to warn the residents to take shelter from the approaching storm, and he always walks that particular stretch of beach.

Some of the old-timers will tell you that this is the spirit of a man who was actually named Gray and who lived near Cape Point in the late eighteen hundreds. He had drowned in a late, sudden, and unexpected storm on that beach. They say he never fails to give his warning, and he is never wrong about the coming storm. He is just as dependable as a barometer.

He is known as a friend and is nothing at all to be afraid of. He loves his people, and he wants to protect them from harm.

Although she is not old enough to remember Gray when he was alive, Mrs. Gene Austin of Hatteras Village has heard Guardsman Brooks tell of the apparition many times. So has Miss Mae Austin of the same village.

"He was one of us in life, and he is one of us still" is the way most of the people think of him.

3

The Affair at Brownrigg Mill

NTEREST IN WITCH-
craft, the exorcism of evil spir-
its, and the occult in general is
nothing new. Mankind has long
been fascinated by and deathly
afraid of witchcraft. The early
history of our country is dotted
with accounts of people who
were suspected of being witches or warlocks and of the
court trials of those unfortunates by their superstitious
peers.

It is thought that the colonial preoccupation with
witchcraft began in 1692 with the hysteria of the famous
witch trials in Salem, Massachusetts, and then spread elsewhere. In those days there was a very large and well-
established trade route by sea between all New England
and the Albemarle section of North Carolina, especially
the principal port of Edenton, better known then as the
Port of Roanoke. It was probably through this commercial and social intercourse that the people of eastern North

Carolina became acquainted with the superstitions and horrors of witchcraft.

Although there were in North Carolina, as elsewhere, special laws against witchcraft and its practice, most historians do not believe that Tar Heels ever went to the lengths of their fellow colonists in persecuting those thought to be witches.

The historian Francis Lister Hawks states the opinion that no one was ever tortured to death for witchcraft in North Carolina. John Lawson, North Carolina's first surveyor general and a historian par excellence, wrote that the only executions he had heard of in North Carolina during this period were a Turk who was convicted of murder and an old woman who was tried and convicted for witchcraft.

In the General Court of Oyer and Terminter in the year 1697, an indictment was brought against Susannah Evans of Currituck Precinct, which reads: "She did, on or about July 25th, last past, devilishly and maliciously bewitch and by the assistance of the devil inflict with mortal pains the body of Deborah Bonthier, whereby the said Deborah departed this life, and also did diabolically and maliciously bewitch several others."

In a shining example of the good sense of the common folk of North Carolina, the grand jury which received that indictment returned it to the court on the same day with the word IGNORAMUS written across the face of the bill. Susannah Evans was discharged by the court and went her way, a free woman. It is privately reported, however, that from that day, some people walked a rather wide circle around Susannah whenever they met her on the road.

As early as 1710 a woman in Chowan County brought a lawsuit against another woman for saying "You are a witch and I can prove it." Apparently the defendant could not prove it, for the court found for the plaintiff in the sum of two hundred pounds sterling for damage to "fame and reputation."

Thus, while there was no recorded wave of hysteria and witch hunting in the Old North State, as contrasted with some of the other colonies, there persisted a fear of the unknown and a desire to have no part of such occult goings-on, if, indeed, they really did exist.

There is one story of witchcraft, however, that is so well documented and established that it has been told, by grandfather to grandson, for a good two hundred years.

To begin with, the location of the story, Brownrigg Mill, really did exist. A part of it is still standing today for the curious to examine as they wish. The mill is located in Chowan County, just twelve miles north of the ancient town of Edenton. It was built in 1762 by Richard Brownrigg, who resided at Wingfield. In the Chowan County Courthouse in Edenton there is recorded the order of court permitting Brownrigg to build this mill. It is found in the minutes of the July Term, 1762, and reads, in part, as follows: "The Petition of Richard Brownrigg, Esqr., for building a mill on Indian Creek GRANTED; the land on one side belonging to the petitioner and on the other to William Boyd, Esqr., who being present in Court, agreed that the said mill might be built, and at the same time agreed that one acre of his land should be set apart for that purpose, for the use of the said Richard Brownrigg."

Richard Brownrigg built his mill well. It stood in active use for almost two centuries, serving mankind with regular operation and with a dependability seldom matched. Generation after generation of people in eastern North Carolina have known and loved that mill (in later years sometimes called Dillard Mill), and they have been nourished by the fine, white meal it produced for their tables.

The old mill, in its busy days, consisted of a sawmill and a cotton gin at one end of the dam across Indian Creek. On the other end of that dam were the corn and flour mills. The large millstones used in grinding the grain were especially quarried and honed at Aesopus on the Hudson River. To the north of the mill, in a beautiful, shady grove of trees, stood the miller's cottage. It made quite a picture in the days when the mill was in operation. The wide, mysterious millpond was rimmed on the far side by cypress trees, ancient even then, whose dark shade lent an air of foreboding to that end of the pond and contrasted sharply with the cozy little cottage nestled in its grove at the other end.

This, then, was the scene during those years immediately preceding the American Revolution, when the mill was operated by a young widower named Tim Farrow. Tim had loved his wife with all his heart, and when she died, leaving him with a very young daughter to care for and raise all by himself, he was distraught. He loved his little girl, and he spent as much time with her as he possibly could, trying to be both father and mother to her. He did a passably good job at it, too, as the child blossomed and grew and began to take over some of the household chores. Yet in spite of their love, it was always lonely in that picturesque cottage with just the two of them.

In addition to being an expert miller, Farrow was also adept at the many other skills necessary to civilized living in those colonial days. He was an expert lumberjack, and he kept not only his own woodshed filled with prime firewood for the winters but those of some of his nearer neighbors also. He owned a double-bitted woodsman's axe of which he was very proud and which he kept honed to razor sharpness. He made the woodsman's claim that the firewood he cut would warm him twice—once when he cut it, and again when he burned it in the large fireplace in his cottage. The magnificent, silver-colored axe was kept in the mill on a shelf over the area in which he stored the corn.

In those days it was the custom of Tim Farrow, when his work was all caught up in the afternoons, when the mill was secured and the sun was beginning to sink behind the huge millpond, to spend an hour or two fishing in the deep water adjacent to the milldam. Fine perch and catfish abounded in those depths. Not only was it a pleasant pastime for him, but it also frequently provided a delicious and nourishing supper when his lovely daughter cooked up the fish just as he liked them.

As he fished, his eyes would often stray to the remote woods on the other side of the millpond. These were deep woods where few people had ever been, and they always seemed to Tim to have an ominous air.

One hot, midsummer afternoon, just as the afternoon haze was turning into dusk, Tim was preparing to end his fishing for the day. As he wound up his lines, he looked far across the pond and beheld a canoe gliding gracefully out of the forest shadows and onto the glassy surface of the pond. The figure of the canoeist was that of a woman whom Tim took to be elderly, since she was dressed in a long-sleeved calico dress and wore a deep poke bonnet pulled forward so that it hid her face completely.

Filled with curiosity as to what sort of elderly woman would be emerging from that dark and mysterious place, Tim waited on the dam and watched the small craft approach, heading directly for him. As the bow of the canoe touched the dam, Tim reached down to help its occupant up onto the walkway. At that instant he realized to his amazement that the traveler was not an old person but the most beautiful young woman he had ever seen in his life. Her hair, when she took off her poke bonnet, proved to be a lustrous, shiny jet black, and the cheeks the bonnet had shaded were peach pink. Her eyes were a deep shade of emerald green and sparkled with life and vitality. She leaped with a lithe grace from the canoe to the top of the dam, holding onto Tim's sweaty palm all the while. When she thanked him for his help, her voice proved to be deep and throaty. Tim was altogether smitten with the lovely and totally unexpected apparition.

When she asked for food and lodging for the night, the fascinated miller immediately agreed. Travel by water was much more common in those days than travel by the uncertain roads, and it was more or less expected that rural householders would put up such a traveler for the night as an act of common courtesy.

Well, the upshot of that meeting was that Tim fell

desperately in love with the beautiful stranger. She spent that night in the spare room at Tim's cottage and the next day moved to the home of a nearby widow lady to spend a few days before continuing her travels. But Tim had seen her beauty by candlelight and across his rude dining table. He had seen how tenderly she looked at his daughter and how the two seemed to hit it off right from the start. He came to realize how much grace and charm she added to his home and how much a woman's touch could mean to his orphaned daughter.

Before the day of her scheduled departure, Tim had paid his court to the beautiful, mysterious lady and had been accepted. The two were married the next time a visiting preacher from Edenton visited the neighborhood. After the wedding, the two settled down in the miller's cottage near the mill.

Tim was ecstatically happy. His new wife and his daughter soon became fast friends, and the young bride introduced them to a whole new world of ways they had never heard of before. She cooked strange and delicious dishes for them and seasoned the old and familiar ones with spices and herbs she bought from traveling peddlers. She used the fine meal Tim brought from the mill as it had never been used before, and her accomplishments soon earned her quite a bit of fame (and jealousy) among the neighboring wives.

At night, around the hearth fire, she would tell wonderful tales and stories that sent cold shivers along Tim's spine. She spoke of ancient Egypt and its Pharaohs as though she had actually been present in those Old Testament times. She was, indeed, an extraordinary person, and Tim's happiness knew no bounds.

Then things began to change.

As the weeks wore on into months, the neighboring housewives began to talk about her. They would say she was a strange one and no one really knew who she was or where she came from, anyway. Then what seemed to be a noticeable pattern of retribution sprang up.

The livestock of those families who had been most open in their criticism of Tim's new wife began to sicken and die from strange and unexplained causes. When some of these women persisted in voicing their suspicions, members of the families became ill and died as though an epidemic had stricken the countryside. The doctors were unable to diagnose or cure these strange illnesses, and a quiet terror began to grip the community.

They began to call her a witch.

It was remembered that she had been seen walking down the lane past the pasture the very week before one farmer's cow had mysteriously died. In another family the grandmother had suddenly contracted an unknown illness and had lingered for days, delirious and speaking in tongues, before she died despite the doctor's efforts to save her. In her delirium, she spoke several times about that "strange lady" stopping in front of the house and adjusting her bonnet, all the while staring fixedly into the front door.

These and other misfortunes were all laid at the door of the newcomer, and it was pointed out that only the people who had been the most critical of her were the ones visited with disaster. People were frightened. They were up against something their doctors did not seem to know how to cope with, and they felt defenseless. No one knew who would be next.

The widow lady with whom the pretty traveler had stayed while Tim was courting her recalled that, on several occasions during those few days, she had gone into the girl's room to clean up and had found the huge feather bed undisturbed except for one large round spot mashed down in the middle of the bedspread, just as though a huge cat had slept there.

Some of the men even went to Tim at his mill and complained of the situation. The bolder ones even demanded that the woman be sent away from the community. Tim just laughed and called them superstitious fools. He indignantly refused the pleas to have the preacher try to exorcise the evil spirit the next time he visited. He most certainly would not put his wife through such a humiliating experience, even if the preacher would agree to try to do such a thing.

Time continued to wear on, and the situation did not get any better. For Tim it got much worse. He grew angry with the people who were calling his wife a witch, and he told them so in no uncertain terms. They, in turn, grew angry with him, and many began to take their grain to another mill, even though it was farther away and did not grind as fine a meal as did Tim's.

Then things began to go wrong at the mill. The young miller would open the mill in the morning and find that the sacks of grain he had stored so carefully for the next day's work had been split open and the grain scattered about the millhouse floor. On other occasions he would find that the sluice gates in the dam had been opened so that the dam wasted water, when he distinctly remembered closing the gates the night before. In the hopper that fed the grain into the grinding wheels, he began to find nails that had sifted down between the stones and caused them to buck and tremble and spit sparks at him and to grind unevenly, thus producing an inferior meal. The bear grass thongs with which he bound the tops of the meal bags were found scattered about the floor, and some of them were thrown into the millrace, even though Tim was always very careful to keep them sorted and in place, ready for use.

Tim concluded that some of his neighbors and former customers were trying to ruin him, to drive him into bankruptcy and, thus, out of the community. He told his wife that he intended to lie in wait for them. He wanted to catch them in their meanness and give them a good whipping to teach them a lesson. Some people were continuing to bring him their custom, but business was badly off and he said he needed to put a stop to all the neighborhood foolishness once and for all. He felt he must clear up the situation if his business were to survive.

Worst of all, Farrow was now convinced that his young wife had grown tired of him and did not love him any more. She seemed dispirited and distracted most of the time, and she would stare at him through narrowed lids with those haunting green eyes. He felt a terrible sense of anxiety and fear, as though some awful doom portended for him or for the whole community. He tried his best to dismiss this feeling by blaming it on the conduct of his neighbors, but the feeling of an unknown dread remained, just the same.

He felt threatened, terribly threatened, and he did not know by what or whom.

For a full week Tim sat up every night at his mill, but nothing at all happened. No bags were ripped open, no bear grass thongs were disturbed, and the mill remained just as it was. Farrow was completely baffled. How could they have known he would be lying in wait for them? Maybe the persecutions had ended. Maybe his neighbors were now going to leave him alone. He gave up his nightly vigils and began to spend those nights at home.

It was about three days after he had given up his watch when a tremendous thunderstorm began to build up in the western sky. Obviously it was going to be a very stormy night, not fit weather for man nor beast, but Tim saw it as a golden opportunity. Now, he thought, if they are ever going to come back, this is the night. They will be sure that I will not venture out in this coming storm and, if they mean me ill, they will try their mischief tonight.

So, just as darkness fell and the storm approached, Tim told his wife that he was going to the store and that he would not be back until quite late, but when he left the cottage, he went to the mill. There he hid himself among some bags of meal he had ground the day before, and there he lay in ambush for the people who had been tormenting him.

Soon after he had ensconced himself, the storm broke with all its fury. The lightning flashed brilliantly, and the thunder rolled and crashed ponderously and magnificently. The mill shook with the reverberations of the squall, and for a moment, Tim had fearful thoughts for his dam and its safety. He could not remember whether he had opened the spillway gates to take the pressure of all this extra water off the dam. However, the storm soon abated temporarily, and the moon broke briefly through the driving clouds.

At that precise time a hoot owl alighted on the roof of the mill and gave an ear-splitting scream that almost startled Tim out of his wits. He jumped so vigorously that he knocked over one of the concealing bags of meal and had to rehide himself. Just then he heard a muffled, pounding roar coming closer and closer, and he half raised himself from his squatting position in anticipation of attack before he realized it was a farmer's wagon rattling over the mill-race bridge in a late evening effort to get home before the second storm broke over the countryside.

Then, and just as suddenly, he heard a horrible cacophony, as though all the frogs in the world had suddenly let loose with their best notes. There were frogs of all sizes, apparently, and notes of all ranges and volumes, a veritable full symphony of frog noises that were ear-splitting. With a shock, Tim realized that he had never heard that many frogs in all his life, and he remembered that, in the folklore of his time, frogs were always associated with witches and demons of all sorts.

As the amphibian tumult continued, the millhouse began to be invaded with lightning bugs, the biggest and the brightest that Tim could ever remember seeing. They came in scores and in hundreds, lighting up the interior of the millhouse with an eerie half-light that, with the frog noises, lent an air of other-worldliness to the little mill.

To the northwest, the thunderous grumble of the approaching second half of the big storm could be heard. The young miller began to regret that he had ever come to the mill. Almost anything would have been better than this awful experience.

And then he heard it.

There came a deafening, drumfire series of blows upon the front door of the mill. It sounded as though a hundred broomsticks had begun to beat upon the door, demanding admittance. Faster and faster the beat rolled on, and louder and louder and more imperative was the demand for entrance! The frog noises seemed to redouble. Then, with a deafening roar of thunder, the skies seemed to open, and a deluge of rain began to pour upon the little mill.

In stark terror, Tim braced himself for whatever was to come.

The battered front door burst open with a bang, and in flew fifty or sixty of the biggest cats anyone has ever seen. Their fangs were bared as though in great anger, and fire seemed to flash from their green eyes. As though on signal, they began to circle Farrow at full speed, howling and spitting and glaring at him. Every once in a while one would break from the narrowing circle surrounding the terrified miller and would strike at him with extended claws, sometimes inflicting deep cuts in his face, at other times ripping his clothing.

Young Farrow had expected nothing like this. He could not fight the enraged cats with his bare hands, and yet he must do something or he would be dead—and that in a very few minutes. Already he was beginning to feel weak from loss of blood. You can't fight wild cats with a bag of meal, and Tim had provided himself with no weapon.

Glancing up in desperation, the young man beheld his trusty double-bitted axe with the razor-sharp blades. The handle was just protruding over the edge of the overhead shelf. Grasping that axe in determination at least to defend himself, he once again faced the cats going around and around with such speed now as to make him dizzy. With a tremendous effort, Tim took aim at the biggest and wildest looking cat in the attacking horde, and he swung his axe with all his might and with a strength born of desperation.

His aim was true. The sharp axe completely severed the right front paw of the huge cat. The severed foot fell into the hopper at Tim's side, and the axe, on the tremendous follow-through of the swing, embedded itself deeply into one of the supporting timbers that held up the roof of the mill.

With a howl of pain and rage, the huge cat burst through the back door of the mill and, with its leg spurting blood, ran along the top of the dam in the pouring rain. All the other cats, with howls and screams, followed the injured beast along the dam. Although weaponless once again, Tim ran after the feline horde, but he stumbled and fell, and the cats vanished into the darkness and the storm.

Tim then ran back through the mill and up the path to his little cottage. Upon bursting into his bedroom door, he found his wife, with her jet black hair and her beautiful green eyes, lying upon the bed, her right hand cut off at the wrist and blood staining the coverlet of the bed.

In horror, Tim looked as she turned once again into a

huge black cat and, spitting defiance at him, leaped down from the bed and limped out through the open door.

Tim's thoughts flashed once again to his beloved mill. Running back in desperation to open the gates before water pressure broke the dam, he was about halfway across the dam itself when the threatened structure gave way. At least a hundred feet of that dam washed out with a thunderous roar, and Tim went with it. A search party recovered his body the next day several hundred feet downstream, and they all wondered at the look of terror on his handsome young face.

The dam was restored after that, and the mill was put back into operation, but they say you can still see the section that was washed out under the huge pressure of the storm and who-knows-what else.

The survivors?

Well, Tim's young daughter was taken by an aunt who lived in Edenton, and although it was a long time before she recovered completely from the shock of that last night, she eventually grew into a lovely and talented young woman and made a good marriage with the son of one of the old families in that colonial town. Her descendants live there to this day, but they shall remain nameless in this account for obvious reasons.

As we saw, the mill was reactivated, the dam was repaired, and a new miller was obtained to run the business. No more mishaps or pranks occurred, although several years later a large, black, three-legged cat showed up at the mill. It would look the miller in the eye with its large, beautiful green eyes and would purr with contentment when the miller noticed it.

The new miller did not like the cat, however, and he did all he could to discourage it from staying at the mill. He was just not one of those people who like cats, and besides, he had heard the story of poor Tim Farrow many times, and he did not believe in taking chances.

When all his rebuffs to the cat did not work and the feline kept hanging around, he knew he had to take decisive steps to remove the threat of a repetition of the Tim Farrow story.

The miller had a fine, muzzle-loading shotgun of which he was very proud and with which he was very skilled. He loaded the barrel of the gun with silver money, dimes and half-dimes, putting an extra large charge of powder behind the load. Taking dead aim at the large cat sunning itself on the dam runway, he fired away and scored a direct hit with at least a portion of the silver.

With a scream of rage and pain, the cat leaped up and ran off into the forest, apparently none the worse for the shot but finally convinced that it was not wanted thereabouts.

So far as has been reported, it has not since been seen in that vicinity.

4

The Little White Cloud

OT FOR NOTHING HAVE the Outer Banks of North Carolina come to be called the fishing capital of the world. Nature seems to have outdone herself to provide just the right habitat for the production of trophy-sized fish of many varieties. Many world record fish have been taken on hook and line in these waters.

One big reason for this piscatorial abundance is the configuration of the region itself. From the icebergs and frozen seas of the Arctic, a stream of very cold water called the Labrador Current sweeps southward along the Atlantic coastline some miles offshore. Up from the tropics, meanwhile, the warm river-in-the-ocean known as the Gulf Stream pushes steadily northward, also just a few miles offshore.

In the open sea just off the point of Hatteras, these two mighty ocean currents come into violent collision, and the resultant giant upwelling of plankton and other minute ocean life creates a fountain of abundant food for all marine creatures. This attracts thousands of small fish, which, in turn, attract other thousands of larger predatory fish, until the whole sea hereabouts abounds with life of all kinds.

Now, this point of collision is not a stationary thing. It changes from location to location depending on the winds and the tides and the ever-changing relative strength of the two currents. Always, though, you can find it somewhere off the point of Hatteras. Equally predictably, you can almost always find another unique phenomenon in the neighborhood.

High in the sky above the point where the two currents join, you will see on a clear day a stationary little white cloud. No matter how clear and unobscured the rest of the sky, nor how fine the weather, the little white cloud is almost always right there marking the spot. Of course it cannot be seen during a storm or during extremely over-cast and cloudy weather, but as a general rule it is there all by itself, sometimes when there is not another shred of cloud in the entire sky.

Scientists tell us that this is a natural phenomenon caused by heavy condensation when the two colliding currents meet. Climatic conditions are usually just right for the for-mation and what they call the "nourishing" of that lonely little white cloud.

The older Outer Bankers can give you a better explana-tion.

They remember the story their grandparents told them of the terrible storm and shipwreck in this "Graveyard of the Atlantic," when all on board the pre-Revolutionary schooner *St. Francis* were lost, with the exception of one handsome young Spanish lad who was washed ashore on Hatteras, more dead than alive.

Around their open hearthfires on a winter's night they will tell their own children and grandchildren how a beautiful young Indian princess named White Cloud, a member of the Hattorask Tribe, found the young survivor. She tenderly nursed him back to life and to health with many wonderful Indian cures and treatments, and the young patient and his benefactress fell hopelessly in love with each other. White Cloud thought she had never seen any human so handsome and so wonderful. The young sailor was also completely enamored of his princess.

Plans for the wedding were made, and the consent of the Hattorask Chief was obtained. But first the young Castillian wanted to make a return visit to his native Spain, there to claim a modest inheritance waiting for him. He wanted to return to his wedding with enough capital to set up housekeeping with his young bride in the European manner rather than the primitive Indian manner.

The Hattorask braves transported the bridegroom-elect to Portsmouth Island, where he signed on board a sailing ship for the trip to Spain. White Cloud waited at the Indian village of Hattorask and began counting the moons until her lover's return.

As her vigil continued, weeks lengthened into months, and months dragged on into years, and still her prince did not return.

Nor did he ever. White Cloud never learned what had happened to him, but she kept up her patient wait all her life long. Finally, when she lay on her deathbed and the

Great Spirit, in pity, asked what one thing she would like most of all, she was ready with her answer. Most of all, White Cloud replied, she would like to continue her vigil for all eternity or until her lover came back in fulfillment of his vow.

The little white cloud always hovering off the point of Hatteras is the spirit of the princess, waiting, faithfully waiting, for the ship that will bring her lover back to her.

And I like that explanation much better than I do the scientific one. It causes me to look at that lonely little white cloud as a long-time and very dear friend.

5

The Dram Tree

I N T H E H A R B O R A T
Edenton in North Carolina
there stood, literally for centuries, a magnificent cypress
tree. This tremendous specimen
stood all alone out in the harbor,
several hundred yards from the
nearest shore and exactly on the
thirty-sixth parallel of north latitude. It was the most
prominent object in the entire vicinity and was a landmark, a sort of landfall, for Edenton harbor.

In colonial days there was much trade between Edenton, which was then called the Port of Roanoke, and
places such as Boston to the north and the Caribbean Islands to the south. The harbor there was usually crowded
with tall ships from most of the ports of this hemisphere.
There were several inlets then in the Outer Banks of
North Carolina, and access to the open sea from Edenton
was relatively easy.

The giant tree was there when Edenton was first settled as an outpost in Indian territory. It witnessed the

building of the Governor's Palace at Edenton and the sumptuous Governor's Mansion at nearby Edenhouse. Governor Eden himself passed the landmark many times as he traveled by luxurious barge from his home to his office.

The tree saw the famous Cupola House built, and it was there when artisans lifted the spire of St. Paul's Church. It was a witness to much history that was important to our state and to the fledgling nation. For instance, the huge landmark was right there in the harbor on the day of the Edenton Tea Party, that event from which many historians think the Boston patriots got the idea for their own tea party. It saw the brave ladies of Edenton empty their tea caddies and pour the beloved tea onto the ground rather than submit to the exorbitant tax the British crown was imposing, and it heard their vows not to drink tea again until the tax was removed.

Our cypress also saw the invasion of the Union fleet under Commander Flusser during the Civil War. As a matter of fact, the occupying squadron used the tree as a landmark and a bearing point to guide them into Edenton harbor.

But however much history the tree witnessed, it was more important than a mere landmark to the seafaring folk of that day. Since the beginnings of the Port of Roanoke, it was known as "the dram tree."

It was the custom of each arriving ship to stop near the tree before entering the harbor, to put a small boat overside, and to carry to the tree a fresh bottle of the finest Jamaica rum and leave it there in a large hollow place in the trunk of the tree. Each ship leaving the harbor would also stop near the tree, and all hands, officers and men, would visit the tree and drink a "dram" of the rum for good luck on the upcoming voyage.

To fail to stop at the dram tree when leaving the harbor was unthinkable. It was tantamount to inviting the worst kind of luck. There were numerous tales of heedless skippers who had failed to stop and whose ships were becalmed in the "doldrums," so feared by sailing men, where there was no possibility of movement for days and weeks on end and the very surface of the sea began to stink as though it were spoiled.

But if failure to stop on the outgoing tide was bad luck, to omit the visit and the gift when arriving at port was to do nothing less than invite disaster. In seamen's tales of those who flouted this custom, the ships were frequently lost with all hands in a violent storm, or else sank and were lost from some other mishap.

As can well be imagined, the tree was much beloved by many people, both ashore and afloat. The residents of Edenton saw their long-expected boats stop there and were afforded a few minutes to prepare a fitting welcome. Many an anxious wife walking the "widow's walk," that railed walkway built on the topmost roof of many colonial houses, got her first news of a returning loved one when she saw a familiar ship stop near the dram tree and put out a dory to visit the cypress.

So far as recorded history tells, there was never a time when a ship called at the dram tree and found the bottle empty or insufficient. It was an obeisance to the gods of the sea as well as the expression of heartfelt wishes for a safe return from the impending voyage.

As is true with all earthly things, the dram tree could not last forever. It weathered many a hurricane and winter's blow. Periods of draught were of no consequence, as its feet were permanently in the water, with fish swimming about its base.

In the winter of 1918 there occurred one of the most severe and unusual storms ever to strike eastern North Carolina. The very sounds and bays froze up so solidly that people could walk and drive teams of horses upon the ice. Many wharves and the pilings of piers and fish houses were ground up by the ice as though they were toothpicks, and water traffic was brought to a complete halt. There was no fishing, no boating, no water activity at all.

Then, when the ice did begin to break up, it came down the sound like a mighty glacier, leveling everything in its path. Bridges and railroad trestles were swept away, and the mighty dram tree, patriarch of the ages, was snapped off at its base by the irresistible pressure of the ice pack.

It fell with a tremendous crash and later sank beneath the surface of the water, where it remains to this day. It lives in the memory of the residents of that area and in their legend. Some Edentonians can even take you to the very spot where it continues to lie, an apparently permanent refuge for hundreds of little fish.

6

Currituck Jack

HE WAR OF THE AMERI-
can Revolution dragged on into
the late seventeen hundreds.
The British redcoats still oc-
cupied New York, and the British fleet still maintained a fairly
effective naval blockade to the
south, including the coast of
North Carolina. Coastwise trade of the colonies was se-
verely curtailed, and our fledgling navy was badly in
need of the supplies and naval stores that eastern Carolina
had in such abundance.

Up in Currituck County, near what is now known as
Currituck Courthouse, there lived a middle-aged man,
Caleb White, a devout Quaker and an American patriot,
who was also a skilled shipbuilder by profession. He not
only built beautiful and seaworthy vessels, but he sailed
them as well, carrying vital cargoes up and down the coast
in the face of the blockade. This was his contribution to
the American war effort. Admittedly it was profitable,
but it was also exciting, and it allowed him to satisfy the

demands of his patriotism without violating his religious beliefs.

The business was not without its risks. In 1778 White had lost one of his finest ships when it was captured and confiscated by the British blockade, and that was painful both to his pocketbook and to his seaman's pride. He always believed, did Caleb, that if he had been in command of that ship, she would never have been captured. But all that was in the past.

In 1779 Caleb White joined in a partnership with his cousin, Henry White, and they set out to build another blockade runner that would be capable of slipping through the British stranglehold, both because of her speed and because her low profile would make her very difficult to see. But they also had the pressing duty of designing and building the perfect shipping vessel, one that would be sufficiently broad of beam to accommodate a large cargo.

In the fall of 1779 she was completed and ready for the sea, and she was quite a thing of beauty to behold. Christened the *Polly*, she was a two-masted, schooner-type ship built with loving care out of juniper and cypress and heart-pine wood. She was broad of beam, but with relatively little freeboard, so that she would lie low in the water. Her jib boom extended a little farther than was usual in ships of her size, which gave room for the extra jib she would carry. This extra sail was calculated to give her greater speed and maneuverability and to counteract her broadness of beam.

Below deck, just abaft the mainmast, there was a comfortable cabin complete with bunks and a little cookstove. Two large hatches on the deck gave access to the cargo holds below, and over these were stout hatch covers whose outer surfaces were tarred canvas. Her hull, masts, and spars were painted black, and her sails were dyed dark brown. She would be hard to catch and even hard to see in poor light.

The two partners, Captain Caleb and cousin Henry White, watched with pride as she slid down into the waters of the North Landing River just a short distance upstream from where that river empties into the waters of Currituck Sound. Caleb was determined to command the *Polly* himself and not risk her fate with someone less experienced at her wheel. To lose this ship to the British would just about bankrupt him. Henry White, for his part, was in complete agreement with the plan. He had a sizable investment in the *Polly*, as well as an equally strong desire to help the struggling colonists win their war of independence. Henry was too old to go seafaring, but he was perfectly content to trust his investment to the skilled hands and eyes of Captain Caleb.

Now, cousin Henry White was a man of considerable wealth by the standards of that day. Not only did he own several large farms, but he also had inherited from an uncle, several years before our story, a young African slave boy named Jack. This lad was said to have come from the Watusi tribe and to have been kidnapped by a Yankee trader and sold to Henry's uncle in the slave market in Charleston. The purchaser took an almost immediate liking to the boy, and he raised him more like a son than a servant. When Henry inherited Jack at the uncle's death, he continued the kind and considerate treatment Jack was used to, and the young fellow grew into one of the finest physical specimens ever seen around Currituck County.

He was nearly seven feet tall, as were his ancestors, but the physical development he achieved was outstanding. He weighed nearly three hundred pounds, but there was practically no fat on him. He was broad of shoulder, narrow of waist, and as quick as a cat on his feet. He could run faster and lift greater weights than any man around. He soon developed into a local celebrity.

Along with his magnificent physique, Jack had developed a personality and a character that were equally fine. He had flourished and prospered under the kind treatment he had received, and his quick mind had eagerly absorbed all the education his owners were able to furnish him. With this he combined a gentle nature and a kind and loving regard for all around him. He was fiercely devoted to his new country and was just as proud of her efforts for freedom as any man was. Jack was a sincere patriot.

You see, the young man had an even deeper interest in freedom than did most men. He was, after all, a slave himself. Though his two owners had always been generous and fair with him, he wanted very much to be free. He longed to be free to remain in this blessed land and to set up his own home. He wanted to marry his own wife and raise his own family and make his own way in the world.

Understanding this universal longing to be free, Jack's original owner had set up for him on the books of his business what was called a "manumittal account." Henry White had continued this account after he inherited the boy.

The practice, which was not at all unusual in the area

at the time, consisted of an arrangement whereby a slave could actually "buy" himself back. Any time a slave rendered an unusually meritorious service or had to work unusually long or demanding hours, he was given credit on his manumittal account. If he preferred, he could have Christmas gifts and birthday presents and other occasional gratuities credited as a money credit on the account rather than receive them in cash or in kind.

In time this could, and often did, mount up to a sum that was equal to the purchase price formerly paid for the slave with, possibly, a small amount of interest added. When this occurred, there was a great ceremony of manumission, or freeing, of the person involved. Official records were entered at the courthouse or nearest seat of government. They proclaimed and gave public notice that the manumitted individual was henceforward and for all time a free and independent person with the right to own property (including slaves of his own), to make contracts, and in all other ways to conduct himself as any other free man.

Although still in his twenties, Jack had accumulated quite a respectable sum in his manumittal account, and the community where he lived took it for granted that he would eventually earn his freedom and that the respected black would soon take his place in the fabric of coastal life as a free man.

Henry White trusted the young slave so completely that he assigned him to sail with Captain Caleb White when the *Polly* undertook her maiden voyage. Jack knew navigation as well as anyone his age, and he was perfectly at home on shipboard.

Small as she was, the *Polly* would need three persons to

sail her efficiently. The third crew member was eventually found in the person of one Samuel Jasper, who was also an accomplished waterman and was about Jack's age. Although not nearly a physical match for the large slave, Sam was strong and alert, and he was a man of temperate habits and judgment. He was also Captain Caleb's brother-in-law and a much beloved member of the family.

A fine crew for any vessel: Captain Caleb, the able-bodied brother-in-law, and the huge and powerful Jack. All hands were satisfied that the *Polly* was not only well found but well manned also. At last they were ready to tweak the nose of the British lion.

And thus it was that the schooner *Polly*, loaded with naval stores of pitch and tar and turpentine, with barrels of corn, and even with a few bales of dried yaupon bushes to furnish tea for the ladies of the blockaded cities, was ready to undertake her first attempt to help break the enemy blockade.

February 14, 1780, the day of departure, dawned cold and overcast. There was a definite threat of snow, and a gentle breeze held steady from the west. Captain Caleb, Jack, and Sam Jasper were all aboard early, as they wanted to catch the favorable tide for their journey down the sound to the open sea. The families and a few friends were on hand to wish them godspeed and a safe voyage. There were firm handshakes all around and a few bearlike embraces, and the three mariners went aboard the *Polly*, which was moored at "the Launch," where Tull Bay empties with a fair flow of water into the North Landing River.

A single jib was raised to pull the *Polly*'s head out into

the current caused by the ebbing tide, and she was on her way. As she cleared the Launch with Captain Caleb at the wheel, Jack and Sam raised the mainsail, which filled beautifully with the westerly breeze. Responsive to her helm, the *Polly* headed proudly out across the river in the general direction of Knott's Island, following the well-known channel to Currituck Sound.

A few flakes of snow began falling as they ran their easting down and raised Halfway Point on their port beam. The wind increased, as did the snow, as they turned now more southerly and sailed out onto the broad expanse of Currituck Sound. They had decided to sail out into the Atlantic through Caffey's Inlet, near where the present community of Corolla is located. Oregon Inlet was not in existence at that time, and Hatteras and Ocracoke Inlets were too well patrolled by the British for them to risk running the blockade at either of those two inlets. The wiser choice and the closer route was through Caffey's Inlet, unmarked though it was.

None of the crew felt any misgivings about the weather. They knew this water as they knew the backs of their own hands, and once out onto the Atlantic, the plan was to sail at least forty or fifty miles offshore to avoid the blockade before turning north to run parallel with the coastline. This last heading would be by compass bearing and by dead reckoning, and no one was better at that type of sailing than was Captain Caleb White.

Down the sound they sailed in high spirits, joining now and then in singing sea chanties, with Sam doing an intricate sailor's jig for the entertainment of the others. It was not yet time to begin their regular routine of one man at the wheel, one man to tend the sails, and one man asleep belowdecks.

The favorable breeze grew fitful and the snow increased as they neared Caffey's Inlet. What breeze there was continued to hold fair, however, and they glided through the difficult channels of the inlet under a full set of sails just as darkness fell. This met Captain Caleb's plan exactly. With this timing, one of the most dangerous parts of the trip would be made under the cover of darkness. So far, so good.

On they sped into the gathering darkness. The bow of the *Polly* began to rise and fall as she met the long, even ground swell of the North Atlantic, the pathway to beleaguered Boston but also largely a British sea. Britannia still ruled the waves, by and large, and her capable seamen were determined to choke the life out of the American uprising.

As she began to make her first long easterly run to get sea room, the *Polly* began to encounter patches of fog. The full moon shed only a ghostly light over the ocean as it settled lower and lower, the fog all but blotting out its beauty. It was reduced to an indistinct, silvery blob in the sky, useful for determining the approximate directions but furnishing no illumination to speak of.

Already running without lights to avoid detection, the *Polly* was almost completely concealed. Thus she gained not only an added measure of protection, but she incurred added danger as well. Simply because she could not be seen, she ran the greater risk of being run down by any passing ship that happened to be on a collision course with her route eastward.

All that night she ran before the faint westerly wind with Jack at the wheel, steering entirely by the ship's compass. Captain Caleb was sound asleep in the little cabin. As there was little need to change the set of the sails during the entire night, Sam Jasper employed himself in restacking the firewood piled on deck. From time to time he would pause in this chore and talk with the helmsman. Forward progress was extremely slow, and the night was bone-chilling cold.

The next day, February 15, began with a heavily overcast sky and a wind that shifted to the northeast during midmorning and increased steadily. The fog bank drifted away to the south, where it hung like a great gray wall under the leaden sky. All that day the *Polly* ran into the wind and drifted under shortened sail as the wind grew stronger and stronger by the hour. As though to add to their difficulties, a freezing rain began to fall, and the little ship labored as she met the increasing waves almost head on. At sunset it was determined not to sail through the night, since they were already well out to sea. Instead, it was decided to heave the *Polly* to and ride out the night while all the three-man crew tried to get a good night's sleep in the warmth of the little cabin.

A drogue, or sea anchor, was put out to hold the *Polly*'s bow into the waves and to make her ride more comfortably and safely. This consisted of several oars and pieces of firewood lashed together into a sort of raft that floated in the water and was secured by a line to the bow of the schooner. Being lower in the water and not so much affected by the wind as the ship was, the drogue drifted more slowly than the boat and thus held the line taut. The line, in turn, tended to hold the bow of the ship pointed directly into the waves. Of course, the ship then drifted southwestward, but at a very slow speed, and Captain Caleb was sure that he had plenty of sea room. Every two or three hours, one of the crew would come up on deck to check the way the *Polly* was riding and to see that all was well.

On that very same night, and unknown to anyone aboard the *Polly*, the British man-o-war *Fame* was also hove to for the night and was also riding at a sea anchor and drifting slowly southwestward. She was part of the blockade fleet, but she had gotten badly off course during the winter storm, and her captain was afraid she might be too near Cape Hatteras for safety. He prudently decided to wait until daylight before continuing his southerly course for Charleston.

H.M.S. *Fame* was a splendid fighting ship of some fifteen cannon and a complement of British marines in addition to her own smartly trained crew. She carried a veritable cloud of sail under fair weather conditions, and she was considered to be a most able vessel for blockade duty. Nobody aboard the *Fame* knew then that just a few miles to the leeward, the American schooner lay dead in the water with only bare rigging exposed to the gale.

Of course, riding higher in the water and with a great deal more rigging and masts and spars exposed to that gale, the *Fame* was drifting faster than the *Polly*, and so the gap between the two was gradually closing as the night wore on.

"Sail, ho," cried Jack from the masthead to which he had climbed to free a snarled pulley, and "Sail, ho," sang out the watch from the mizzentop of the man-of-war.

Both ships exploded into frantic activity.

The two ships had sighted each other at the same instant, and at the time of the sighting no more than three miles of open water separated the two crafts.

It was obvious to Captain Caleb when he had focused his telescope on the warship that she was a British blockader, and it was equally obvious to Captain Maher of the *Fame* that he was looking at a fat prize of a blockade runner. Both the hunter and the hunted knew what they must do.

Neither captain bothered to retrieve his sea drogue but cut it loose in his haste to pile on sail. Both wanted to get under way with as much headway as possible just as soon as possible. The *Polly* was downwind from the *Fame*, so her best bet was to turn "on her heel" and run for all she was worth. Captain Maher knew instantly that his best course was to give pursuit until he could bring his intended prize within range of his bow gun.

In a gale such as was developing, the *Fame* had all the advantage. She carried more sail and higher sail than did the *Polly*, and Captain Maher felt confident that if he did not swamp his boat under the added sail, he could overtake the fleeing schooner. True, a stern chase is always a long chase, but he felt he could pull the trick off with prudent increases in sail area and patience in slowly overhauling his prey.

Captain Caleb, on the contrary, felt that if he could keep his lead for several hours, he might be able to duck into that fog bank he had left the day before, if it were still there. Then, he thought, he could take evasive action and elude the Britisher.

Most stern chases are indeed long chases, and this one proved to be no exception. The *Fame*, while she gained steadily on the *Polly*, did not overtake her with the speed Captain Maher wished, and the little schooner managed to find the fog bank and slip into it before the man-of-war's cannon could be brought to bear.

Captain Caleb White had won the first round.

Now, trying to outguess the other captain, Caleb spun the wheel and headed the *Polly* on a southeasterly course, thinking that the Britisher would assume that the *Polly* would run under cover of the fog for the protection of the shore and would chase after her in that direction.

It would have been better for the three shipmates if she had indeed run for the shore.

After sailing for several hours at top speed in that south-easterly direction, the *Polly* burst from the fog bank and into clear weather, only to find that the *Fame* had duplicated her maneuver. The British ship had, unknowingly, run a course parallel with that of the *Polly* until she had approached within a few hundred yards off the *Polly*'s port beam. And there the man-of-war was, boiling along "with a bone in her teeth" and still upwind from the *Polly*.

The jig was up. At least it was up as far as the race between the two vessels was concerned. A well-aimed shot from the British ship whistled across the *Polly*'s bow, and another came even closer as it whined beyond the schooner and splashed into the sea. Thus, obviously within cannon range and having nothing to fight back with, the only course for the Americans was to heave to and await the command of their captors. The *Polly* was a prize of war, and her three-man crew was captive.

A boarding party from the warship was not long in coming. The *Fame*'s jolly boat came dancing over the waves, rounded the stern of the little schooner, and then threw grappling hooks over the starboard rails. Up and over the rails and onto the heaving deck of the *Polly* came the crew of the jolly boat, followed by Captain Maher himself.

You see, both skippers had been correct in their strategy. Captain Caleb was correct in guessing that Captain Maher would assume that the *Polly* would make a run for shore. That's exactly what the Britisher did think the probabilities were. What the Carolina skipper did not know was that Maher did not know exactly where he was. A clumsy midshipman had dropped the captain's sextant five days earlier, and as a result, all Maher could be sure of was that he was somewhere off the Virginia Capes. He did know that the dangerous Platt Shoals lay somewhere to his south, and beyond that lay Wimble Shoals, and then, most dreaded of all, Diamond Shoals. It was no flight of fancy which had named that area the "Graveyard of the Atlantic."

The British skipper had no intention of taking the risk of running the *Fame* aground and having her break up around him. He was well aware that he would have less chance of catching the *Polly* if he headed the *Fame* to the southeast, but he also knew he would be running less chance of losing his ship to the stormy shoal water. He wanted sea room for his vessel first of all. Second, he wanted to capture the *Polly*.

As the fates decreed it, he got both his wishes. There the *Polly* lay on the surface of the stormy sea, scarcely two days and less than a hundred miles into her maiden voyage, and she was a captive, a prize of war.

After inspecting the captured ship as best he could in the squally weather, Captain Maher detailed five of his men to stay aboard the *Polly* as a prize crew and sail her to New York, which was still in the hands of the British forces. Her naval stores could be put to good use in maintaining the warships based there, and her corn would help nourish the occupying troops ashore.

Captain White, Currituck Jack, and Sam Jarvis were placed in irons brought over from the British ship and were then lashed to the mainmast on deck, where they could be kept in plain sight of the helmsman. The five limeys intended to sail the *Polly* to New York with no help from her former crew. She was now a British ship.

With a dip of her colors in salute, the *Fame*, with Captain Maher back on board and now in a very good mood, came back before the wind and sailed off in a southerly direction for the Charleston blockade.

As if in sympathy with the spirits of the American shipmates, both the barometer and the thermometer began to drop steadily. A freezing rain began to fall. The wind, already strong and out of the northeast, gradually increased until it was blowing a full gale and developed into a typical north Atlantic storm. Everyone aboard the *Polly* was miserable and cold.

Later that afternoon the sailor on watch on deck discovered some unusual activity among the prisoners on the foredeck. Upon investigation it was found that Caleb and Sam had almost succeeded in working loose the ropes binding the giant slave. Another five minutes of such effort and he would have been free to move about the pitching decks of the *Polly*. Jack was quickly secured and tied, this time spread-eagle on his back and lying face-up into the driving rain. For further security and to keep that escape attempt from happening again, the other two Americans were herded down into the forehold of the ship, where they were securely tied.

Belowdecks it was cold but dry, and the two white men could feel every pitch and swoop of the laboring vessel magnified several times. Luckily, neither Captain Caleb White nor Sam Jarvis was subject to seasickness. Cold ship's biscuits from the *Fame* and cold water were given to them twice a day, and they were closely watched while they ate the simple fare.

If it was bad in the hold it was pure, freezing hell on that foredeck. With no protection at all from the elements, Jack lay on his back, the freezing rain beating down on his prostrate figure. Every once in a while a breaking sea would sluice along the deck, bringing even more misery. It would have killed an ordinary human being.

All afternoon long and all that interminable night, the giant black man suffered through torture few men have had to endure. From time to time a thin coating of ice would form on the outer garments of the huge prisoner as the freezing rain continued to fall in a steady downpour.

The *Polly* was making no progress at all. The weather

was just too rough, so the British seamen were content to let her ride, as before, at a sea anchor and with no sails set. The little vessel continued to lie there on the surface of the troubled sea, just waiting out the storm until conditions were more favorable.

The next morning, when Jack was brought his breakfast of cold bread and water, his captor broached the subject of forsaking his American colleagues and joining the British cause. After all, the British seaman argued, Jack had known nothing but slavery at the hands of Americans, and he was in his own present miserable condition because he had thrown his lot in with the colonists. It was an attention-getting argument.

All that morning the prize crew took turns talking with Jack, always in the same vein. "Come over to us," they pleaded, "and we can promise you a warm cabin and good food for now and your own freedom when we reach New York." "The American cause is doomed," they argued. "At most, all you can expect from them is continued slavery. With us, a man of your strength and skills could join the Royal Navy and make a wonderful career for himself. We can get the Royal Governor of New York to make you a free man as soon as we reach that city." And so on and so on, all through that forenoon, as Jack's misery grew and the chill invaded his very bones.

Jack would have been less than human if he had not considered their arguments. After all, he was a slave. Freedom, his own personal freedom, was something he had longed for all his life. If only he could believe these sailors, believe that freedom was now his for the asking. Could he turn traitor to his friends and his adopted country?

What Jack could not and did not know was that this was a standard British trick used literally hundreds of times in usually successful efforts to persuade slaves to run away to the British. Once their loyalty was gained, the men were not freed at all. When their usefulness to the British cause had been served, they were sold back into slavery, usually under much more severe conditions than the ones they had left. The invaders treated them as so much captured contraband.

Jack began to think back upon his own life as a slave. He remembered how he had hunted and fished with these shipmates of his and others in Currituck. He recalled how he had been treated more like a brother than a slave or even a servant. He thought of how he had been given the opportunity to better himself with such education as was available and how he had the opportunity to earn his own freedom, which, as a matter of fact, he had almost accomplished through the manumittal agreement.

Jack held in his breast a burning desire for freedom, but his desire went further than his own personal affairs. He wanted freedom for his country also. When he had earned his own freedom, he wanted it to be a freedom in a free land where every man is as good as every other man. He wanted to be truly free.

This slave, this Currituck Jack, was in his own way as much a patriot as any man who ever lived. With a wisdom beyond his years and an insight that transcended his times, he decided to stick with his friends and his adopted country.

Jack didn't let his captors know his decision, however. He told them that he would seriously consider their suggestion and would pray over it and let them have his answer before they reached the port of New York.

In belated concern for his health and to show their "sympathy" for him, the prize crew moved Jack that afternoon back down into the dry darkness of the hold where his two shipmates were being held. They tied him tightly even then and secured the hatch as tightly as they could. After all, a slave dead from exposure would bring them no profit in the slave market.

There in the darkness the three friends began to discuss their condition. Jack told the others of the pressures put upon him to defect and join the British and how he had told them he would let them know his answer soon.

The shipmates agreed that therein lay their best and possibly their only chance to recapture the *Polly*. It was agreed among them that Jack would pretend to go over to the British and would offer to help them work the ship as they proceeded northward. Once he gained his freedom he was to look for a chance to free his comrades and join with them in an effort to recapture the *Polly*.

Their decision was made. For warmth, the three Currituck County men lay down as close to each other as their bonds would allow, and they fell into a fitful sleep. They needed their strength for the fight to regain their ship. If they died in the attempt, they would die with honor.

Even Captain Caleb White, devout Quaker that he was, was in complete agreement with the plan, although he hoped in his heart of hearts that there would be no fatalities. His mind was filled with admiration for Jack and the tremendous courage the young man had shown. He had always been fond of the huge black. Now he was more than proud to be associated with him in this daring undertaking.

By the next morning, Jack was burning up with fever. His day and night of exposure to the cruel elements as he lay tied to the deck of the *Polly* was beginning to take its toll. There were times when he was incoherent and other times when he was completely out of his head. In between times, though, he had periods when he was rational, and he insisted on going through with the plan. There was a calculated risk as to whether he would unintentionally reveal the plan in a moment of delirium.

When the prisoners were brought their breakfast, Jack asked to be taken to see the midshipman who was in charge of the prize crew. He was able to convince the British seaman that he had seen the light and had finally realized that his own best interest lay in siding with the British in exchange for his freedom.

So convincing was Jack and so sincere did he seem that the midshipman ordered him released from his bonds and allowed the freedom of the ship. If he mistook the light of fever in Jack's eyes for fervor for the British cause, no one can blame him. After all, Jack put on a wonderful and convincing show. He repeated all the arguments his captors had made to him.

That very day the storm began to abate and the wind began to subside. Plans were made to get under way the next morning. The prize crew gave Jack the task of carrying the food to his former shipmates in the hope that he could induce them to defect along with him. It was on one of these trips into the hold that he was able to slip Captain

Caleb a sharp knife the slave had taken from the galley. Also on that trip he managed to leave the hasp securing the hatch unfastened so that it could be raised from underneath. Jack, you see, had now become one of the prize crew and was allowed to sleep in the cabin.

At dawn the following day, the weather had abated still more. Although a large sea was still running, conditions looked good for resuming the voyage of the *Polly.* During the night, the prisoners belowdecks had used the knife to good effect, both in cutting the ropes that bound them and in picking the locks of the irons in which they had been placed. The hour for action had arrived.

Overhead, the patter of feet on the deck was unmistakable as the prize crew went about weighing the sea anchor and bending sails onto the yards. Captain Caleb and Sam felt the difference in the roll and pitch of their ship, and they knew she was beginning to come under control of her wheel and the pull of the sails, which were being hoisted. Now, if ever, was the time. Now, while all hands were busy bringing the schooner on course.

With all their combined strength, Caleb and Sam managed to throw back the hatch cover onto the deck from beneath, and they came leaping up to the deck. Caleb made straight for the wheel, where the midshipman was trying to bring the schooner onto her assigned course and was fighting the big wheel with all his might. Without more ado, Caleb hung a roundhouse swing flush onto the jaw of the youngster. His blow had all the desperation of a man fighting for everything he held dear. Caught completely by surprise, the midshipman went down and out like a light.

63

Simultaneously, Jack seized a marlinespike from the fife rail at the mast and lit into the two shipmates who had been helping him raise the bulky mainsail. In a matter of seconds, the two heads were laid open to the skulls and the two figures lay writhing on the deck.

In a perfectly coordinated move, Sam attacked the sailor who, far out on the jib boom, had been attempting to free the outermost jib. Climbing out after the Britisher, Sam wrapped his legs around the jib boom just abaft the dolphin striker and applied a stranglehold with his arms wrapped around the neck of the astounded sailor. He pressed the sailor's head up and against the jib boom until he felt the form grow limp in his grasp. Then, instead of just letting the body drop into the sea, Sam laboriously inched his way back down the jib boom, dragging the limp body of the crewman with him until he reached the deck. Throwing him into the scuppers, Sam then turned to assist Caleb, who was struggling with another member of the prize crew.

The surprise was complete. The Englishmen, very much the worse for wear, were herded by Jack, brandishing a bloody marlinespike, until they were all confined belowdecks in the very forward hold that had been the prison of the Americans. Needless to say, they were all securely tied up, and the hatch cover was double-checked to see that it offered no opportunity for opening from beneath.

Back in control of his ship, Captain Caleb White ordered the British flag taken down and safely stowed in the cabin.

Knowing that they could not possibly reach Boston

with Jack as ill as he was, Caleb ordered him belowdecks to the cabin and to bed while the *Polly* was put on a course that soon brought her to a safe anchorage at Annapolis, Maryland.

By that time, Jack was completely out of his head from pneumonia and frostbite from his long exposure. He was tenderly carried ashore, and arrangements were made to have him admitted to the hospital at Annapolis, where he lingered between life and death for several weeks.

Finally, however, his magnificent physical strength began to assert itself, and under the care of doctors, he regained his right senses. More than a month later, he was dismissed to go home.

Meanwhile, the Continental Congress, hearing of Jack's bravery and self-sacrifice, passed a resolution expressing its appreciation and its admiration for his bravery. It even asked that he be made evermore a free and independent citizen of the country he loved so much.

Tradition tells us that, upon his return to Currituck County, Jack not only was freed and made a citizen of his state and country but was given all the money that had accumulated over the years in his manumittal fund.

Tradition also tells us that he used this money to buy the freedom of a very pretty and wholesome black girl whom he had long admired. After he freed her, he married her and settled down with his own boat and his own nets and his own small farm in his beloved Currituck County.

The old folks in the area still talk about Currituck Jack. When some youngster gets overly proud of his strength or his speed or his bravery, the oldsters will tell him the tale of Currituck Jack and how he was not only a physical giant but a gentle and brave American patriot as well.

Currituck Jack is a true and genuine folk hero to the people of our coastland. In the minds of many, he was also one of the finest and least-heralded patriots of our young country.

7

The Legend of Old Buck

ANY BEAUTIFUL LEG-ends and customs surrounding the Christmas season have grown up in this country. Some customs, such as the Christmas tree, festooning the house with mistletoe, holly, and pine, and the singing of Christmas carols, have been adopted from other lands. All Christmas traditions are lovely, and all have roots in recorded history, but none is more interesting or more truly American than the legend of Old Buck, which is told and retold along our Outer Banks as each Christmas season approaches.

You see, the Bankers celebrate two Christmases each year, one on the largely universal date of December 25 and the other on January 6, or "Old Christmas."

Until the year 1752 the entire Christian world celebrated Christmas on January 6. In that year, however, the new, or Gregorian calendar was adopted in England, the mother country of America, and the day on which Christmas was celebrated became December 25. In the British

Isles this was accomplished by royal edict, and relatively little difficulty was experienced in making the transfer. If the king wanted to move Christmas Day around, that was one of his privileges.

With characteristic stubbornness and the independence that was already becoming a trademark, the American colonists refused to go along with this newfangled calendar. For years thereafter they continued to hold to the old or traditional calendar, and they went right on celebrating Old Christmas on January 6. Gradually, however, as the colonies gained their independence and as trade and commerce with other nations increased, the new calendar, which had won worldwide acceptance, replaced the old, and the new Christmas became customary. This was true over most of the new nation, with the exception of certain isolated places where tradition and custom play an especially important part in the lives of the people.

Such a place is our Outer Banks of North Carolina, which for years was isolated from the rest of the nation to a great degree. The Hatteras Island town of Rodanthe is an excellent case in point. Although the people are completely modern in every respect and are used to all the "advantages" of modern-day life, they still appreciate and observe their ancient customs with a wonderful sense of history.

We still celebrate Old Christmas in Rodanthe on Hatteras Island. Although the official date is still January 6, the actual big celebration and public participation are always held on the weekend nearest to January 6, in order that children of the island who have had to move away and live their lives in other places may be able to come back on that weekend and participate in the beloved customs of their childhood once again. And they do come back. From hundreds of miles away they come and take up the skeins of yesteryear. Then, when the nostalgic weekend is over, they return to their homes and jobs refreshed, overfed, and confirmed in their belief that they come from the finest spot on the face of this earth. Christmas gifts are exchanged, and gargantuan feasts of oysters, crabs, fish, and other seafood go on at all hours of the day and night.

Along with this traditional observance of Old Christmas, there has grown up a body of local or regional legend that complements the season and heightens the enjoyment of both old and young celebrants. Tales and customs have persisted over the generations and have become treasured traditions in themselves. One of the most beloved and best remembered of these inheritances is the story of Old Buck.

To get to the beginning of the story, we must go far back into history. The genesis of the legend of Old Buck lies in the folklore of England.

From the dim recesses of English history comes the story of Saint George, patron saint of all Britain, who slew a terrible dragon and thus delivered the country from its domination. One colonial version of that legend has it that, as Saint George was about to administer the coup de grace to the monster, the dragon pleaded most pitifully that its spirit, at least, be allowed to survive.

Moved by the tearful pleas of the conquered dragon, Saint George agreed to spare the spirit of that creature on condition that he forthwith leave England and never,

never return in any form or fashion. To this the dragon agreed, and he immediately went screaming off on a gale of wind to northern Europe. There he wandered for many hundreds of years, sometimes taking the form of a timber wolf and at other times appearing as a giant bear, but true to his vow, never did he return to England.

And now the mythological scene shifts sharply.

In the middle of the sixteenth century, Don Carlos Montiero of Spain was in deep trouble. A respected grandee of the kingdom, his name had been connected with a plot to overthrow the monarchy, and although it had never been proved and he had vehemently denied it, he was in disfavor with the king. The penalty for treason, as everyone knows, is death, and for a while it looked as though Don Carlos would pay that ultimate penalty. However, partly because the crime had never been absolutely proved (Don Carlos had covered his tracks well) and partly because he was, after all, blood cousin to the queen, the grandee's life was spared. It was spared on condition that he and all his immediate family be exiled from Spain and that he take up residence in the new land across the sea which Ponce de Leon had discovered for Spain back in 1513.

With heavy heart but grateful that his life and his possessions had been spared, Don Carlos went about the months-long preparation for his removal to the New World. A large and seaworthy galleon was purchased, and all the family's treasured possessions, all their gold and silver and jewelry as well as all their masterpieces of the painter's and silversmith's arts, were carefully stowed

aboard. Also loaded aboard the ship were the family records and the magnificent dueling swords and armor that
Don Carlos had inherited from his father, Don Lowen-
burg. Also placed in the galleon were large casks of ancient wines and a generous supply of the favorite foods of
Spain that would keep without ice on the long sea journey
that lay ahead.

At last everything was in readiness for the departure.
The mighty galleon rode low in the water under her
burden of cargo. Every inch of storage space had been
used, with some of the cargo even lashed in place on the
decks. Don Carlos had even considered purchasing another galleon to lighten the load of the large vessel, but
in the end, he decided against it. Instead, he invested that
money in the purchase of the largest, the most beautiful,
and the meanest-tempered fighting bull he could find in
all Spain. The old grandee was a bullfighting enthusiast,
and he saw the chance to start his own line of fighting
bulls in this new land, where he understood the climate
was ideal for the raising of cattle in general and fighting
bulls in particular.

The bull they finally found and purchased for the new
life in the New World was a marvel indeed. Named
Bucca, he was the offspring of the finest line of fighting
bulls. He was born with a mean disposition and a love
for combat. A magnificent physical specimen, he was a
good deal larger than most fighting bulls, but with a cat-
like quickness that belied his huge size. Dreaming of his
own line of such splendid animals, of his own bull ring,
and of becoming the bullfighting king of all the new

"Land of the Flowers," Don Carlos almost became reconciled to leaving his beloved Spain.

Bucca was lowered, on the day of departure, down into the hold of the galleon, where a space in one of the walkways was somehow made for him to stand. An ample supply of hay was placed nearby, and arrangements for bedding him down were accomplished. Bucca was held by a nose-ring attached by a heavy chain to one of the uprights belowdecks, and a large tub of drinking water was placed before him. During all this introduction into completely new surroundings, the giant bull was remarkably docile and cooperative. He had made no resistance even when he was hoisted high in the air with a belly sling and then lowered into the darkness of the 'tween decks of the galleon.

Unknown to any human, at this time the spirit of Saint George's dragon was looking for another animal to take possession of. In a manner known only to dragons, he was aware of the splendid animal in the hold of the galleon, and he also knew the plans of Don Carlos. It looked like an ideal situation for him, so without more ado and with a cry of triumph, he invaded the body of the bull.

At the instant of this incarnation, the Monteiro family had been at sea for only a week and were making steady and uneventful progress toward their anticipated new home. Their first inkling that there was anything unusual afoot came when there burst through the ship a half-scream, half-bellow that sounded as though all the hounds of Hades had been let loose aboard the ship. This awful noise was followed immediately by the sounds of what can only be described as complete bedlam from below—the noise of timbers breaking and containers being upset and tossed about the interior of the hold, and the screams and shouts of terrified seamen.

Bucca had, indeed, flung a fit. Hot breath plumed in gasps from his nostrils, and his eyes gleamed like living coals in the darkness of the belowdecks. The wreckage there was almost complete. Barrels had been burst, containers and tubs thrown about, and the whole area was in disarray. It took seven brave men armed with pikes and boat hooks to subdue him, but they finally managed to get several lines around Bucca and tie him to the deck. There he continued to snort defiance and roll his angry red eyes at the sailors. Saint George's dragon had found a new home.

Several days later the weather became stormy, and the ungainly galleon had to alter course to maintain her headway, steering somewhat to the north of the direction originally planned. Soon the weather went from bad to worse, and the little party of expatriates found itself in the clutch of a mighty hurricane roaring up from the Carib Sea with awesome and deadly power.

The gales shrieked louder and louder, and the seas grew greater and greater. There were literally mountains of dark green water threatening to engulf the wallowing galleon with each huge wave and dropping it sickeningly down into the chasm at the bottom of the troubled trough. At times the whole sky was blotted out, and all that could be seen were those terrible walls of tortured water reaching seemingly up to the sky on every side. The next moment the ship would be perched on the very top of a surging mountain of water, and then would come another sickening, sudden drop. All the while the ship groaned and moaned as if it were in mortal pain and agony and about to wring itself to pieces.

And that is exactly what happened. With one last shuddering moan, the valiant ship burst her seams, turned over on her beam-ends, and sank gradually beneath the tortured surface of the sea, leaving a sodden mass of wreckage floating on the troubled waters.

Now it so happened that the two youngest sailors on the ship had been assigned the task of trying to feed Bucca and keep him supplied with water. They had done their very best to do this, although they were in terror of the huge beast after he turned wild. Although frightened, they had managed to shove water and food within his reach and had tried to keep the decks in that dark hold as clean as possible with long-handled mops and pails of sea water.

It also happened that all the people on board that ill-fated galleon were drowned in that awful storm and shipwreck. All except those two youngest sailors. And Bucca. Somehow the mighty bull had managed to free himself, or he was freed when the ship broke up. He swam about the wreckage-strewn surface, bellowing loudly and tossing his mighty head from side to side as if trying to sense in what direction safety lay.

In one last desperate struggle, the two young sailors managed to make their way from hatch cover to floating spars to tangled remnants of masts until they reached the free-swimming bull. There each grasped one of the cruel horns of that animal and hung on for dear life.

Strangely, the bull did not attempt to free himself from their grasp, nor did he try to hurt them in any way. Lifting his nostrils as far out of the water as he could reach, Bucca began swimming steadily and with powerful strokes of his legs as though he now knew exactly where he was headed.

How long he swam and why he did not try to rid himself of the extra weight of the two young sailors will never be known. In due time and with all three more dead than alive, the strange companions finally did reach the shoreline at Hatteras Island. Bucca dropped to his knees in the sand in much the manner of a dying bull in the bull ring, but after a few minutes he struggled to his feet and staggered off into the nearby woods.

The two sailors, exhausted and nearly unconscious, lay face down on the wet and stormy beach, gasping for breath and unable to sit up or to help themselves. Finally they were found by a hunting party of Indians, who took them to their camp and revived them with scalding hot yaupon tea and vigorous slaps about the head and face. Finding the Indians friendly and intensely curious about these pale-skinned visitors from the sea, the two gradually learned to communicate with them, first by sign language and then by the spoken word.

The Indians believed without question the wild story of the arrival of the newcomers. The sailors were looked upon as some sort of minor gods and were respected and given positions of honor. In time they "married" into the tribe of their benefactors and settled down to a life of ease, waited upon and looked up to by the women of the tribe and considered blood brothers by the braves. Their descendants became some of the first "Mustees" of Hatteras Island—beautiful, blue-eyed, fair-haired Indians who were always treated as special people by the rest of the tribe.

Bucca staggered off into the woods and, in time, recovered from his near-fatal experience. Legend has it that he lives there to this day, spending most of his time in Trent Woods on Hatteras Island.

Bucca, or Old Buck, as he is fondly called by the islanders, has been there now for over four hundred years, and he hasn't hurt anyone yet.

It is not known, of course, whether the shipwreck and his own narrow escape sweetened the disposition of the mighty bull, or whether just living in that salubrious climate and on the same island with those wonderful Outer Bankers has caused him to have a change of heart.

It is known that his main occupation nowadays is keeping rather close tabs on the conduct of the island children, particularly those around Rodanthe and Avon, so that he can report on them each time Christmas rolls around. He is a reliable source for the gift-giving adults who want to know just which kids have been really good for a whole year and which ones may not have been quite so good.

Old Buck faithfully makes his appearance in Rodanthe every Old Christmas, to the delight of the children and to the nourishment of reverie on the part of the misty-eyed older islanders. During the other days of the year you can usually find him in Trent Woods, sometimes appearing as an enormous steer and sometimes in his own proper person as a mighty bull. If you look closely, however, you will always find that old familiar fire in his eyes, the dancelike gait, and the resounding bellow that have become his trademarks.

8

The Beckoning Hands

HE BASINS OF THE ROA-
noke and Chowan rivers were
two of the earliest centers of
civilization in the New World.
Many beautiful homes were
built along their shores, and
towns such as Plymouth and
Edenton played an important
part in the settling of the Province of Carolina, both under
the Lords Proprietors and under the royal governors.

Most of the mansions built along the lovely shorelines
were the creations of planters and import merchants, but
at least one was built at the direction of a famous pirate
who wanted not only a secure place to keep his plunder,
but also a comfortable and gracious showplace where his
noble friends—governors and statesmen and such—could
be entertained in the gracious style to which they were
accustomed. After all, he considered himself a sort of
import merchant, too. You see, even in those days it was
not unusual for some of the more successful criminals to

want to cross the line into respectability for themselves and their families.

The edifice of which we speak is still standing on the top of a small but high bluff overlooking the Chowan River. It was carefully planned down to the last cubic foot. Its masonry walls are very thick, almost like a fort, making it nearly soundproof and very easy to heat in winter and cool in summer. A large basement gives opening to a brick-lined tunnel that descends through the heart of the bluff to a well-concealed door at the level of the river.

This made the unloading of boats a very practical matter, as well as a very private one. No prying eye could possibly see what was being transferred from rowboats to the mouth of the tunnel or vice versa.

The high ground upon which the house is located afforded an excellent lookout both up and down the river, so the occupants had ample notice of the approach of any travelers by water and could take any steps they considered expedient. As most travel in those days was by boat, the beautiful home was indeed a very snug and secure nest.

At the will of the owner, the splendid structure could be either a fort or a gracious palace. It was built by the most skillful artisans and of only the very best materials obtainable from the seven seas of the world. In addition to the stones of which the basic structure was built, there were rosewood, mahogany, and teakwood from the tropics and golden oak from the timbers of captured ships. The house was built with all the meticulous attention to detail and strength that the skilled boatwright is accustomed to putting into the building of an ocean-going vessel. It is still sound and secure down to this very day.

Perhaps the most striking feature of the interior of the mansion was the grand entrance. Here a huge hall was lighted by sterling silver sconces bearing wax candles that blazed brilliantly. A very wide staircase opened just opposite the massive front doors. Made of highly polished mahogany, the staircase swept upward in a graceful flair and opened on an upstairs hall, which served as a passageway to the rooms of the upper floors. Carpeted with fabulous oriental rugs, the hall and stair gave dramatic welcome to the house as one entered the front doors. The rugs are no longer there, but that magnificent staircase still sweeps in its graceful and imposing curve, inviting the guest to enter and explore the regions above.

Large parlors and dining rooms open off this large entrance hall, and in its early days a kitchen was located to the rear of the house, providing easy and direct access to the dining room through a butler's pantry.

The only trouble was that the family of the would-be-respectable pirate would never live there with him.

His lovely young wife did not approve of his piratical ways nor of his affairs with other ladies of the area. But she was also apprehensive about a curse that had been laid on her pirate husband by an old hag who lived in Nag's Head Woods.

It seems he had "pressed" or kidnapped the old woman's son, an only child, into service aboard the pirate ship. The boy had subsequently been killed during an attack upon a merchant ship, and the old crone blamed the pirate captain for depriving her of any hope of grandchildren. In spite of a rather large sum of money given to her by the buccaneer, she swore a curse on his head to the effect that he, too, should never know the joy of being a grandparent, but that his line should be cut off for all time and forever.

It was shortly after news of this malediction reached her that the brigand's wife left him and took their daughter back to her home town of Charleston, South Carolina. She maintained separate quarters in a lovely house there, and the pirate was free to visit her and their beautiful young daughter Caroline.

Several years later, the pirate captain caught a fever in the West Indies and died aboard ship. He was buried at sea according to the custom of the Brotherhood of the Sea, and his faithful first mate then sailed openly into Charleston harbor to carry the news of his passing to his widow. He also carried his captain's sword, other personal belongings, and the shipmaster's share of the accumulated loot, which amounted, in value, to a sizable sum. This, together with her other holdings and previous gifts from her husband, left the widow quite comfortably fixed.

Among the properties inherited by the widow and her daughter was the beautiful mansion overlooking the river, and the two of them soon took up residence there. It was much cooler in the summers, and the winters did not seem to be as piercingly cold or damp. The house was magnificently appointed and very comfortable, and the neighbors on adjoining plantations were what was termed "quality folk." All in all, it seemed a nearly ideal place to complete the rearing of a daughter.

Caroline grew in grace and in beauty and soon was the toast of the entire region. The great stone house often rang with music and merriment as the young folk of the province gathered often for extended houseparties that lasted several days at the very least. Life was pleasant, unhurried, and serene. There was plenty of delicious food, plenty of good and genteel company, plenty of light and laughter, and above all, plenty of time in which to live the good life to the fullest.

Or so they thought.

Youth and laughter and friendship blossomed into love for the beautiful, diminutive Caroline, and wedding arrangements were soon made for her marriage to the scion of one of the oldest and wealthiest families in the entire Roanoke-Chowan area.

The wedding ceremony was to take place at the home of the bride, and invitations went out to all the great and many of the near-great in that whole region. It was to be a brilliant social affair, with the ceremony to be performed by a visiting bishop of the Anglican Church. The house was beautifully decorated with Christmas decorations, for the ceremony was to take place on New Year's Day, still a part of the Christmas season. A string orchestra was brought in from Edenton to furnish the wedding music, and the days preceding New Year's were an endless round of parties and holiday festivities.

The wedding day arrived at last. The Bishop made an imposing figure in his vestments as he stood very erect, prayer book in hand, ready to perform the nuptial ceremony. He and all the other guests were assembled in the great hall. The nervous young bridegroom was in his place beside the Bishop, and the bride was to enter from a dressing room located just off the great hall.

The orchestra struck up the wedding music, played it once, then again, but the bride did not appear. The Bishop cleared his throat and glanced over at the mother of the bride, who was beginning to experience the first symptoms of panic. A chill of premonition gripped her, and she remembered the curse of the Nag's Head hag.

Then, from above the level of their heads, came . . . a very feminine giggle!

All eyes snapped immediately to the head of the huge stairway, and there they beheld the bride in all her wedding finery, looking down at them with twinkling eyes and with a teasing smile on her pretty lips. She looked no bigger than a child as she stood there, radiantly happy and the most beautiful thing the bridegroom had ever seen. In spite of warnings that he must not look upon his bride in her wedding dress until she stood beside him at the altar, the young man could not take his eyes off her.

Tiny Caroline stood there for a brief moment, poised like a bird. She was reveling in the adoration and adulation flowing toward her from her beloved and her friends on the floor below.

Then, with an impish grin and looking directly into the eyes of her fiancée, she taunted, "Catch me and you may kiss me." She tossed her pretty, lace-bedecked head and beckoned to him with both her hands. Turning, she ran swiftly along the upstairs hall and disappeared around a corner.

Accepting the challenge, the young bridegroom leaped forward and ran up the broad stairway, three steps at a time, until he reached the hall above. Then he turned in the direction his beloved had taken and ran down the hallway after her.

There was no Caroline!

Up and down the halls he ran and into all the rooms, and still he could not find his bride. Calling her, he begged her to come out of her hiding place, as the wedding guests were becoming restless and the Bishop was distinctly annoyed at this frivolous interruption of the religious ceremony.

Soon amusement or annoyance turned into genuine concern as the whole wedding party joined in the search for the missing girl. The great stone house was searched thoroughly, and the grounds around the house were carefully explored for hundreds of yards, but without producing a sign of the young girl. No strangers had been seen in the vicinity, and there was no known wild beast thereabouts that was large enough to have carried her off. No boats were missing from any of the piers along the waterfront.

Caroline had just disappeared without a trace.

After several months of futile search, Caroline's bereaved mother closed up the big stone house and moved away. It is said that the mysterious disappearance of her lovely daughter continued to grieve her and stayed on her mind so much that she soon became deranged and would talk of nothing but her lost bride-girl. There is no doubt that her grief shortened her life. The poor, troubled lady died without ever finding out what had become of Caroline.

The very next New Year's night, one year to the day after the strange disappearance, some children in the neighborhood of the great stone house came home badly frightened and told their parents of seeing a ghostly, white face floating and flitting from window to window inside the closed mansion. They said the "thing" beckoned enticingly with two ghostly, white hands. Their frightened parents forbade them to go ever again upon the grounds of the old pirate's mansion. Of course, being children, they did go back, but none of them was ever harmed.

Year after year, always on New Year's night, the pallid face and beckoning hands continued to appear in the windows of the house until the ghost became a local and then a regional attraction. Many brave people tried to solve the mystery of the apparition, but when they gained admittance to the house, the phenomenon always vanished with a long and pitiful sigh.

The old pirate's beautiful home became known as "the house with the beckoning hands," and prudent people avoided it whenever they could. Nevertheless, many upright and reliable people—people of unquestioned sobriety—swore that they continued to see those beckoning hands and that pitiful face, but no one could solve the mystery.

Then, years later, a man who had made a deep study of such things rented the house from its owners to try to get to the bottom of the strange occurrence. Many believed he was a little touched in the head to be searching for a solution to a mystery that had gone unexplained all those years.

He actually moved into the house to try to obtain, first-hand, the feeling and the mood of the place. All by himself, he searched the house from top to bottom again and again. He never actually saw the beckoning hands or the wistful face, but he was convinced that his neighbors were telling the truth.

Then, on New Year's night, after he had waited in vain for the apparition, he fell asleep in the huge feather bed in the master bedroom of the house. As he slept he dreamed a very vivid dream.

He dreamed that he was witnessing that strange, interrupted wedding ceremony of many years before. He saw all the actors in the event as though from a vantage point above and beyond the wedding party, so he could see all of them at one time.

In his dream he saw the bridegroom leaping up the stairs in pursuit of his young, lovely bride, and he saw tiny Caroline turn and run down the hall in mock fright from her beloved.

And then he saw it. As Caroline dashed along the hall and turned a corner, she lost her balance in her long wedding dress and fell against the wall for support. Her steadying hand reached into a secret crevice in that stone wall and touched a secret lever. He saw a trapdoor open beneath her feet, and he caught the flash of wedding finery as she fell through that trapdoor and into a secret, windowless room beneath. He saw the trapdoor reclose as the heavy stone flooring turned upon its metal pivot and glided into place, locking shut with a metallic click.

In his dream, Caroline was entombed alive! The sheer horror of his vivid dream shocked him into consciousness, and he awoke with a scream.

Did his ears betray him or did he hear the high-pitched cackle of an old hag? As he rolled from his bed, the first light of a winter dawn was breaking over the eastern sky.

Without more ado, but trembling as if he had an ague, our researcher went directly to that portion of the hall he had seen so clearly in his dream. The stone wall was still there, and so was that secret crack or joint between the stones. Pushing his hand wrist-deep into the aperture, he felt the end of a rusty metal lever which, with great exertion, he was able to move.

Slowly, slowly, and with a great groaning sound as though it were reluctant to reveal its secret, the huge stone in the floor began to swing on its now rusty pivot until it stood fully open. A vagrant beam of sunlight fell directly into the opening before him.

There, on the floor of that secret room, he beheld a tiny human skeleton, almost as small as a child's, the bones of both hands extended along the floor in a beckoning gesture. On the head of the skeleton there was a trace of ancient white lace, almost like snow upon its brow. The wedding veil of lovely Caroline.

And thus was the mystery finally solved. The remains of poor Caroline were given Christian burial, and the treacherous trapdoor was sealed shut so that it could never again imprison an unsuspecting traveler along that hallway.

The beckoning hands?

Well, most of the people in the neighborhood will tell

you that they disappeared from that day on, but there are others who will tell you that they can still be seen, but only on a dark New Year's night. They are beckoning, ever beckoning.

9

The Jobellflower

LL UP AND DOWN North Carolina's Outer Banks, from Caffey's Inlet in the north to Portsmouth Island in the south, a visitor may see at certain seasons of the year literally millions of the blossoms of a beautiful orange-yellow flower. Known botanically as *Gallardia*, this lovely flower grows in great drifts in the sand of the flats, as well as at the bases of the huge sandhills. Nowhere else that I know of is it found in such spectacular profusion. The legend of its presence is told in one of the most poignant bits of folklore that persists along the Outer Banks.

Back in the early days of the twentieth century there lived a man named Joe Bell who was married to a very lovely lady named Josephine Bell. She was lovely in mind and in heart as well as in body. Very deeply in love, these two middle-aged people liked nothing better than to spend their summers in the then-undeveloped region already known at the time as the Outer Banks.

These shores were almost untouched by civilization in those days. Aside from the fishing villages, most of which were back on the sound shore, there were only the life-saving stations and a few rich men's hunting clubs, which were accessible only by boat. In the main, the hunting clubs made scarcely a ripple in the usually serene and happy lives of the native fishermen. A few Bankers worked as caretakers for the buildings and as guides during the hunting season, but that was about all.

It was in this idyllic region that Joe and Josephine Bell were privileged to spend their long summer and fall vacations. They lived mostly in private homes but insisted upon paying their way as they went. They were loved all up and down the Banks.

Josephine was especially well known for her kindness and helpfulness to the women of the region. Almost as skilled as a midwife, she was always ready to help when a child was about to be born or some sickly Banker lady needed a little attention.

Joe was his wife's right-hand man in all these situations. He was never too concerned with his own pleasures to find time to run errands and to help around the house, if in no other way than to comfort and reassure the expectant father. No wonder they were welcomed whenever they appeared. They were, indeed, Good Samaritans. It was a happy thing when one fisherman would say to another, "The Joe Bells are coming" or "The Joe Bells are at our house for a spell."

As all such things must, this wonderful companionship in love finally came to an end. Josephine sickened and died one bitterly cold winter when the couple was at their home many miles from their beloved Outer Banks. On her deathbed, Josephine made Joe promise that, if she died, he would continue to go back to the coast they had loved so well and so long, and he promised to continue helping the natives of the region in whatever way he could.

That next summer Joe returned, as he had promised, but he could never be satisfied to tarry long in one home or in one community. Always on the go, he moved from community to community, and everywhere he went he found memories of his lost Josephine.

The full moon rising out of the Atlantic or the sun setting in a blaze of glory into the sounds was for Joe a sight not only of breathtaking beauty but also of excruciating pain. His sheer loneliness in the presence of so much beauty was almost more than he could bear.

Then, one day when he had paid a quick visit back to his inland home, he found several clumps of beautiful orange-yellow flowers growing in Josephine's garden, where none like them had ever grown before. They seemed to be centered around a huge seashell his wife had used as a garden ornament.

Joe accepted it as a sign, and he knew immediately what he was supposed to do. Carefully digging around each of the lovely golden flowers, he left a ball of dirt around the roots as he lifted each plant from the soil. Then, carefully wrapping them in damp newspapers, he inserted the plants into brown paper bags and carried them back all the long trip to Nag's Head Village. Early the next morning, he carefully set them out in the garden plot of a friend, where they grew and flourished.

From this small beginning Joe Bell began his self-imposed pilgrimage of beautification all up and down the Outer Banks. For Joe Bell it was purely and simply a labor of love. Here, he felt, was a fitting memorial to his beloved Josephine.

Like a latter day Johnny Appleseed, everywhere he went Joe either sowed or set out his beautiful flowers. The flowers took to the climate as though they knew what was expected of them. Everywhere they multiplied and grew and spread out until they became almost a golden carpet when they were in full bloom.

And so they do to this good day. Though sometimes upset and circumscribed by paved highways and extensive construction, they seem to flourish everywhere there is room and people will spare them. They do not even seem to need any special care. If they are just left undisturbed, they will prosper, spreading their seeds on the ever-present winds and extending their carpet of beauty indefinitely.

By the natives, and by others who know, they are not called *Gallardia*. They are purely and simply "the Jobell-flower." Just that one word. And by so naming it, they have memorialized not only Jo Bell but Joe Bell as well.

The memorial of love has outlasted a monument of stone. May they always be called "the Jobellflower."

IO

Rodanthe's Drum of Old Christmas

ODANTHE IS ONE OF that series of little towns that dot the Outer Banks of North Carolina. In some ways Rodanthe is typical of these wonderful places, where fearless people have battled the sea for generations. Their stories of daring in the face of nature's cruel fury are numerous and fascinating, and most of them contain more than a germ of truth. Somewhat corroborative of the truth of many of these stories are the customs that have grown up and have come to be solemnly celebrated year after year by the islanders.

One of the most fascinating of these is Rodanthe's Drum of Old Christmas.

You see, "Old" Christmas is still celebrated at Rodanthe and at other places on the Outer Banks. This observance is the traditional Christmas, which the entire Christian world observed before the introduction of the Gregorian calendar. It falls, by our present calendar, on January 6, and the people of the Banks always celebrate on the week-end closest to that date.

One of the highlights of the celebration each year is the "playing" of the Christmas Drum, an ancient percussion instrument obviously of pre-Revolutionary vintage. It is extremely ancient and weatherbeaten in appearance, and it is patched and repaired at various places. It is still in usable condition and is employed in solemn ceremony on Old Christmas.

The drum has been in the possession of the Payne family, one of the Outer Banks' finest, for many generations. At the present writing it is in the possession of Mr. Louie Bell Payne, who lives in Wanchese but who goes back each year for Old Christmas at Rodanthe, not many miles away. Before he kept and played the drum, it was in the custody of Mr. Dameron Payne, late of Rodanthe and Wanchese, who was the youngest of ten Payne brothers. Each of those brothers, in the order of his seniority, held possession of and performed on the storied drum.

On Dameron Payne's death, his widow, Mrs. Fannie Payne, saw to it that the custom was not broken and that the drum descended to one of the blood. Of course, before Dameron and, in turn, each of his brothers held the drum, it was the proud charge of Mr. Benjamin Payne, and before him, of Mr. William Payne, and there the Payne line becomes more difficult to trace as you go back in history.

All those fine people are dead now, except Mrs. Fannie Payne and Louie Bell Payne, and neither of them will discuss any of the legends that have grown up about the drum. Each of them did give permission, however, for an investigation to be made on Hatteras Island to reconstruct the legend of the drum, and this story is the result of that research. As I had been warned, there were several versions of the story, but this is the one that is most prevalent. At their request, I shall not mention the names of any of my informants, nor shall I identify them other than to say that they are all Outer Bankers born and bred and that they verily believe the legend. I am inclined to believe it, too.

As is the case with so much of our North Carolina history, the roots of this story lie deep in the history of the British Isles, for it is there, in the spring of 1746, that we pick up the story of the drum and learn what it meant and how it came to America.

The locale is a desolate and fog-shrouded moor in Scotland known as Drummossie in Inverness-shire. On the night of April 14 in that year 1746, the Scottish Highland troops of Bonnie Prince Charlie were encamped, preparing for the inevitable battle the next day with the English forces under the command of William Augustus, Duke of Cumberland and son of King George II and Queen Caroline.

Virtually all the clans of the Highlands of Scotland were there ready to battle to the death for Prince Charles Edward. They did not consider him to be a pretender at all, but the rightful monarch of England and Scotland. Nor did they consider themselves rebels, but rather crusaders for the right. They had been moderately successful in other battles with the English. Their fierce, wild charges with claymores, wreaking death and destruction while bagpipes screamed and drum rolls thundered, had stricken terror into the hearts of more than one English soldier. They fought like wild men and they looked like wild men and they were well nigh irresistible.

Present with the other Highland Scots was a lad twelve years of age named Donald McDonald. A Highlander among Highlanders, he would have liked nothing better than to wield his own claymore in the forefront of one of those wild charges, but the elders of the clan had ruled that he was too young. He had been entrusted instead with the Golden Drum of Bonnie Prince Charlie. It was his important duty to sound the alarm when danger threatened and to join with the pipes in sounding the charge for his uncles and cousins and other kinsmen.

It was a magnificent drum. It was a brilliant gold in color, and it flashed in the sun like a jewel. Its snares were of Highland rawhide, and the drumheads were of fine, expertly tanned Highland deerskins. It had a deep, mellow tone, and the sound of it carried for a great distance. The Golden Drum was held almost in reverence by the Highlanders. It was said that it would beat softly, of and by itself, when any danger threatened its owner, and it would play a light and skipping beat whenever good fortune portended.

The morning of April 15 dawned cold and foggy on desolate Drummossie as the battle began. It was a typical Highlander offensive, but this time the Scots found that the English had prepared for them. The British spearmen thrust the butts of their long spears into the ground behind them and held the points at about breast level, thus impaling many a charging Scot on the sharp, slanting point. Then from the rear came shower after shower of yard-long arrows from the accurate English bowmen.

It was a horrible slaughter. The English gave no quarter that day; they had heard that the Scots had intended to give none. What survivors they could see were pursued and put to death by the Duke of Cumberland's men. When the battle ended, more than a thousand lifeless Highland bodies littered the field. On his twenty-fifth birthday, William Augustus, Duke of Cumberland, had won one of the most important and, up to that time, one of the most bloody battles of all English history.

In the height of the battle, Donald McDonald had been struck in the left shoulder by an English arrow. The shaft lodged in his body, with the point sticking out of his back just above the shoulder blade and the butt of the shaft protruding in front.

Aided by a wounded bagpiper, Donald was able to drag himself, leaving a trail of blood, about a mile to the bank of the River Nairn on the Plain of Clava. Here, among the mysterious and huge stone monoliths of pre-historic Scotland, he lay for two days and two nights, unconscious at times and bleeding heavily, until he was found by an old man in a dark gray robe, who ministered to his wounds with herbs and mysterious potions. He broke the arrow piercing Donald's chest and then withdrew it from his body. Eventually, he carried the boy back to his Highland home.

During all this time, Donald McDonald had never relinquished his grasp on the Golden Drum. Part of the wood and drumhead were stained deeply with his blood.

He had drunk of the rainwater that the face of the drum had caught as he lay bleeding on the mysterious Plain of Clava.

The lad found it good to be back home again, but his troubles were not over. Some of the surviving Highlanders had sworn to fight on in the cause of Prince Charlie. The Duke of Cumberland, hearing of it, had begun a systematic hunt to find and kill such persistent rebels.

The Battle of Drummossie, which the British to this day call the Battle of Culloden, marked the end of the Stuart cause. Never again were the Stuart allies able to mount a realistic offensive, although for some ten years thereafter they talked and they dreamed of a renewal of the fight.

In all these dreams the Golden Drum, now to be called the Drum of Drummossie, played an important part. Donald went from clan to Highland clan for shelter and protection as he preserved this symbol of their cause. But the warlike spirits waned, and the persistence of the English hunt for any dissidents reduced their numbers until, finally, all hope was gone. To rebuild his life and to escape the danger of English reprisal, Donald McDonald took ship to the New World, hoping to find in America the opportunity he could no longer have in Scotland or in England. Of course, the Golden Drum of Drummossie went with him as his most prized possession.

The story of the Great Autumn Storm of 1757 has been told too many times to bear repeating here. Suffice it to say that it was one of the most violent and destructive hurricanes ever to hit even that "Graveyard of the Atlantic." It took a horrible toll in lives and property.

It was Donald McDonald's bad luck (or was it really good luck?) that his ship should be caught in the midst of that cataclysm and should roll over on her beam ends and sink within sight of what we now know as Rodanthe.

Donald was washed overboard, still clinging to his precious Golden Drum. He would surely have sunk beneath the surface of that wildly churning sea had it not been for Bonnie Prince Charlie's drum. Clinging to it in desperation, Donald found it to be an ideal life preserver as it lifted him with its natural buoyancy and kept his head above water.

Even so, he would have drowned if it had not been for the keen eyesight and bravery of one of those earliest Paynes, who saw his plight from the shore and plunged into the surf to help the castaway. The suction of those huge waves and the violent undertow associated with the storm almost dragged them both to their destruction, but they finally managed to crawl up on the beach beyond the reach of the heaviest breakers to lie, panting and almost unconscious, in the shallow wash of the water. Donald still clung to his drum.

In the brilliant autumn days that followed, our Scot was nursed back to health and strength by the Hatteras families. He grew to know these stalwart people and to love them for their kindness and generosity as well as their courage and complete honesty. There was much here, in both the people and the rugged land, that reminded him of his beloved Scotland. True, there were no mountains, but there were long, wild, deserted beaches and sand dunes where a man might walk for a day and never see another living human.

And so it was that Donald McDonald found his American home. He spent the rest of his life with his friends, the Outer Bankers, and he became one of them. He married into the Payne family, but God did not bless the marriage with children, so the drum, when Donald died, was inherited by the oldest son of the Payne who had rescued him from the sea. From him it has descended, always in the Payne family, for the hundreds of years since it floated young McDonald ashore.

It is said that the drum retains its magical qualities, which were so well known in the days of Bonnie Prince Charlie.

Old-timers claim that it still beats of its own accord when America, its adopted home, is in danger. You have only to know how to listen for the beat to hear it, faint but clear. Its slow and measured beat is said to have foretold every war the United States has engaged in, and a light and lilting cadence is said to have welcomed every American victory.

It is still a beautiful drum and is highly prized by all the Paynes, as well it should be. The instrument is called by various names, all of which have some relation to the legend of its arrival on these shores.

People call it the Golden Drum of Bonnie Prince Charlie, the Drum of Culloden, and the Drum of Drummossie, but I prefer the Old Christmas Drum of Rodanthe.

II

The Core Point Ghosts

B ATH, NORTH CAROlina, is an ancient town. It was already quite old when the thirteen American colonies declared their independence from Britain. The town itself was an oasis of culture in the New World, and the countryside roundabout was inhabited by prosperous plantation owners, as well as by a variety of wild beasts and usually friendly Indians.

But it was Blackbeard's town as well as the seat of the British government. It had all the characteristics of a frontier village in addition to the indicia of a British outpost. Although there were some thieves and knaves, the great majority of the people were industrious, brave, and honest. They believed in their dream of a new life in a new world where a man's opportunities would be limited only by his industry and his ability, and not by the whim of any tyrant. It was indeed a cradle of freedom. And it was always a pretty and a picturesque little town nestled on broad waters, which were the highways of commerce and travel.

If today you sail down Bath Creek toward the Pamlico River, as Blackbeard sailed numerous times, and if you look dead ahead of you, almost due south across the broad reach of the Pamlico River, you will see a fertile region known as Core Point. This area was also well settled before the Revolution, and on this beautiful point jutting out into the river there lived a wealthy family, who shall remain nameless here, because many of the descendants of that family still live in and around eastern North Carolina and are among the most respected citizens in the state.

At the time our story begins, war fever was running high in eastern Carolina. Young men from the farms and towns were flocking to the colors of the rebellious colonies, and the long struggle for independence had begun in earnest. The idea of a free and independent nation caught the imagination of the colonists, and the vision spread like wildfire.

In the beautiful plantation house on Core Point, the young daughter of its wealthy owner was very much in love with a young swain who lived and worked in Bath Town. He would sail his boat across the river to visit her, and they were often together with the full consent and approval of both families. The young couple seemed ideally suited to each other, and their courtship proceeded without any visible signs of disagreements or even the customary lovers' quarrels. It was a beautiful time for them both.

The twin stimuli of peer pressure and patriotism began to work on the young man, however, and he felt that he must enlist in the armed forces of his beloved land. So off he went to join the men who were so successfully defending Portsmouth Island by hit-and-run naval and amphibious tactics that were centuries ahead of their time. In shallow-draught galleys propelled by as many as twenty oars, the swift-moving and highly mobile force played havoc with the heavier and slower British warships and made life generally miserable for them. The invaders managed to get away with some small quantities of livestock, but they paid dearly for every steer they took.

There was a certain risk, though, and the young Bath resident was unlucky enough to take a British musket ball in the chest. He died a day later and was buried in a hero's grave on Portsmouth Island.

Back home at Core Point, his young fiancée was prostrate with grief. Her whole world had come tumbling down around her ears. She, too, had been caught up in the war fever, and as has so often been the case in wartime, she had loved not wisely but too well. She confided to her mother that she was in a family way and was mortally afraid of what attitude her father might take. And well she might have been.

The outraged gentleman berated her for disgracing his family and for bringing to naught all his lifelong plans for her. No trace of sympathy or pity was evident in the old man. Completely immersed in self-pity and self-righteousness, he thought only about the wrong that had been done him and how he, in his old age, must now pay for another's mistakes.

The mother was torn between love and tenderness for her daughter and loyalty to her husband. In this environment, the young girl almost went out of her mind with remorse and shame.

The whole community took sides in the matter and indulged in a heated argument. Those were the days of rather strict moral codes, even if they were, even then, actually observed as often in the breach of them as in the observance.

The upshot of the whole affair was that the young lady, by the time she had her baby, was almost insane and was completely incapable of thinking coherently. A week after the baby was born, she deliberately smothered it to death and laid the tiny, lifeless body before her father.

She was tried for the murder, was convicted, and was sentenced to hang from the branch of a tree overlooking the river, the very same tree under which her baby had been buried. Why the court thought this to be appropriate we shall never know, but the death sentence was carried out, and she was buried alongside her child.

Down to this day, the residents of the area insist, the double tragedy is regularly brought back to mind on the occasion of each full moon. At midnight, so they say, you can hear the pitiful sobbing of a very young child and then, as if in reply, the sorrowful and frantic cries of the mother as she tries in vain to get to her child and comfort it. The sobbing and crying lasts for about an hour each time and can unmistakably be identified as that of an infant and a woman.

Many people have heard it and continue to hear it. Several have even tried to walk to the source of the sound, but no one has ever come up with any idea or any suggestions as to how to quiet those ghosts and assuage that young mother's centuries-old grief for the awful things that she and her father did. Ask any of the older residents of the south side of the river. They know the story all too well.

12

The Mysterious
Maco Lights

OE BALDWIN WAS A
railroading man and a good one.
He loved to watch the big en-
gines roll, and he thoroughly
enjoyed the excitement and
drama of railroading. Besides, in
those days just after the Civil
War, Joe knew he was lucky
to have any kind of job, much less a good job with the
railroad. The rolling equipment was not in very good
condition, and the line was short-handed, but the trains
ran pretty much on time, and everybody sort of looked
up to a railroading man.

Joe's home was near the southern end of the coast of
North Carolina, in the beautiful port city of Wilmington.
He worked for the Atlantic Coast Line Railroad, now
named the Seaboard Coast Line, on runs into and out of
Wilmington. Joe had worked in railroading all during the
recent Civil War and had reached that degree of pro-
ficiency which brought him the responsible job of train
conductor.

Baldwin took his job seriously, too. He knew full well that the safety of his passengers and of the train itself often depended solely on the judgment and the coolness of the conductor who, with the engineer up ahead in the locomotive, coordinated the train's movements. If the engineer of the train could be called its skipper, then the conductor would certainly be entitled to the rank of first mate.

Such was the situation on that autumn night in 1867 when Joe and his train were homeward bound toward Wilmington. They were approaching a little whistle-stop station, now known as Maco Station, located about fourteen miles to the west of the city of Wilmington. The conductor was taking his ease, his lighted lantern on the floor of the aisle beside him in the otherwise deserted observation car at the very rear of the train. No stop was scheduled for the little depot ahead, and everything was running smoothly and at full speed. Suddenly, and with that sixth sense that is part of every born railroading man, Joe became aware that something was wrong.

His car was not behaving as it should. Instead of the steady clickety-clack of the wheels on the rails, he sensed that the train was almost imperceptibly slowing down. Leaping to his feet, he ran the short distance to the front end of the car. Looking out of the connecting door, he discovered that his car had somehow become uncoupled from the rest of the train, which was speeding away from him into the night.

You see, in those days railroad cars were hitched together by a manual coupling secured by a metal pin. That pin had somehow fallen out and disconnected his observation car, which continued to hurtle through the night under its own momentum, but at a gradually decreasing speed.

Joe's first thought was for the safety, not of himself, but of his train. Good railroad man that he was, he knew that a very fast express train was following his train along those tracks into Wilmington, but he did not know how far behind him that express train was. His own train had not been in any great hurry on this trip but had taken it easy for the entire run.

Grabbing up his lighted railroader's lantern, the conductor ran to the back of his car and out upon the little observation platform at the rear of the car. There, to his horror, he beheld the headlight of the oncoming express train bearing down upon his slowing observation car. His own train, the train to which his car belonged, had by now vanished into the night as it sped on to Wilmington with nobody on board aware that the observation car was missing.

Leaning over the rail of the observation car, Joe Baldwin frantically began to wave his signal lantern back and forth, back and forth, to warn the engineer of the onrushing train about the presence of the obstacle ahead. By now the observation car had rolled almost to a stop on the straight, level track.

Joe never tried to save himself. Right up to the moment of impact he continued to wave that warning lantern. No one knows why, but the people on the express never saw that light. Just before the collision, someone in the cab of the express reached up and pulled down hard on the whistle cord. The wail of that steam whistle filled the whole countryside with its eerie noise.

In the crash that followed, the observation car was almost completely demolished. The overtaking express train was knocked off the track. Its whistle jammed in the wide-open position and screamed, for the better part of an hour, like a tormented banshee.

Joe Baldwin was decapitated. His body tumbled down one side of the railroad tracks and his head must have tumbled down the other, because from that day to this, the severed head has never been found, although diligent search was made of the whole area. Death, of course, was instantaneous.

Joe's lighted lantern, flung upward at the very last second either by the force of Joe's arm or by some freak of the collision, described a glowing arc as it curved skyward and outward and finally descended and came to rest, upright, in the swamp alongside the tracks. It burned brightly there all the rest of that night and until it was removed early the next morning by a railroad worker helping to clear the tracks.

The deceased conductor, or at least part of him, was given a fine funeral and, in the tradition of that day, was eulogized for his bravery and his devotion to duty and to his family. His widow was given a railroad pension, and his grave was marked with a suitable tablet of stone, which stands to this day in a cemetery of the port city.

And then strange things began to happen.

Not every night, but on many nights, there began to appear, alongside the tracks near Maco Station, a ghostly sort of light that looked exactly like a conductor's or brakeman's warning lantern. It would bob along and wave just as though it were being carried by a walking person, and then, all of a sudden, it would go out.

Sometimes the light would suddenly fly up into the air, as if thrown in a skyward arc, and would come to rest on the swampy ground beside the railroad tracks, where it would just go out! People began to try to walk up on that curious light, but it would always evade them and fade away into the distance as they approached.

Of course, the people thereabout soon began to call the light "Joe Baldwin's Light." They whispered that it was indeed Joe Baldwin the conductor looking for his head.

That strange light has continued to occur and to mystify people right down to this very day. So far as I know, it is occurring there right now. It has been viewed by literally thousands of people. For years the young folk of Wilmington had a custom of going out to see the light and to see who had nerve enough to try to catch up with it. A few tried, but none succeeded.

In the year 1873 a new variation of the light was observed. On some occasions not one light but two would be seen, one rushing and overtaking the other light, then both blazing brightly for a second before going out in the darkness.

This variation is seen occasionally even now. No one seems able to explain the phenomenon unless he does, indeed, adopt the theory that it is Joe Baldwin still searching for his head. Several years ago the townspeople got the notion that it might be the reflected headlights from cars on nearby highways, so they organized themselves, got permission from the proper authorities, and on one night blocked off the highways in the vicinity. The light appeared right on schedule. Some of the townsfolk pointed out that there were no highways in that location when the mysterious lights began back in the eighteen hundreds, so blocking the highways had been doomed to failure from the beginning.

For many years several locomotive engineers were scared nearly out of their wits by the sudden appearance of a warning lantern swinging back and forth on the tracks ahead. A number of trains were brought to sudden, screeching stops, which resulted in discomfort to the passengers, until the railroad found a way of coping with the situation.

No less a person than Grover Cleveland, at that time President of the United States, was aboard the Coast Line train to Wilmington one night in 1895 when it stopped at Maco Station to take on wood and water.

Walking back along the tracks to stretch his legs and get a breath of night air, the President observed a trainman carrying not one but two lighted lanterns, one white and one red. Upon asking what possible use the railroader could have for two lanterns at the same time, Mr. Cleveland was told that it was so that the engineers could tell the difference between Joe Baldwin's light and the real danger signal of the railroader. Mr. Cleveland made mention of this occurrence in several of his speeches after that.

In the late nineteen forties, a U.S. Army colonel named Thompson became so interested in the lights that he resolved to settle, once and for all, the question of just what they were and what (or who) caused them.

From the military reservation at Fort Bragg, he brought to Maco Station a detachment of soldiers, machine-gunners mostly, to hunt down the elusive light. Remember, these men were hardened combat veterans from World War II who were certainly not likely to be frightened or "spooked" by any ghost light or, for that matter, any decapitated conductor they might run across. Of course, they said they did not believe one word of the Joe Baldwin theory but would come up with the real causes that produced these effects around the little settlement of Maco.

Well, the first two nights the soldiers were there, the lights did not appear. (There is no telling in advance on just which nights they will appear and when they will not.) The third night, however, the soldiers' patience was rewarded. The swinging single light appeared, traveling its unhurried way along the railroad tracks, even causing a dull reflection on the surface of the rails themselves.

Exultantly, Colonel Thompson deployed his men in skirmish formation—spread out so as to envelop and entrap that light. With nerves tingling with excitement, even these combat veterans felt their scalps begin to tighten and the hair on the backs of their necks begin to stand up in some unreasoning, primordial response to fear of the unknown.

Slowly and deliberately the skirmish line advanced, and just as slowly and deliberately, the mysterious light retreated down the tracks, ever swinging and bobbing as though held in the hand of a man walking steadily along. Then, all of a sudden, the light vanished! The soldiers continued for a few steps and then halted. All was completely dark and completely silent and completely motionless until the soft drawl of a young sergeant from Tennessee broke the tension.

"Look behind us, Colonel," he said. There, to the rear of the line of soldiers and proceeding unhurriedly down the track away from them, was the gently swinging light. The soldiers went back to camp the next day, the Colonel still contending that there was some natural explanation for the mysterious light.

Well, that is the story of the Maco light. It is still there. It still occurs frequently but irregularly, and it still mystifies most people who have seen it.

Sometimes it is a single light bobbing down the railroad track. Sometimes the two lights have their collision resulting in a flarelike arc of light like that from a thrown lantern.

You may prove it to yourself if you like. The people of Wilmington and of little Maco are very hospitable and very courteous, but they have come to take the mysterious light for granted by now. They would be happy if someone would come along and supply a "logical" explanation for these displays, but they are perfectly content just to accept the phenomenon until that happens.

They will help you all they can if you ask them.

But, please, one word of caution. If you do go down to Maco Station to see the lights and you do have the small amount of patience it sometimes takes to wait for their appearance, do as the railroad company says, PLEASE STAY OFF THE RAILROAD TRACKS.

Fast trains still use those tracks, and you certainly do not want to join Joe Baldwin in his search for his head. If you go onto the tracks you are not only taking an unnecessary risk but you just may also be arrested for trespassing.

Play it safe and don't join Joe.

13
The Legend of Mattamuskeet Lake

F YOU STOOD ON CAPE Point on Hatteras Island and if you had telescopic vision and looked almost due west across the fifty miles of beautiful, open water that is Pamlico Sound, you would see one of the wildest and most strangely beautiful areas on the face of our earth.

This is the land known as the deep woods, and most of it is so remote and so inaccessible that the foot of the white man has never trod its surface. Indians may have hunted over part of it, but to the white man it is as unfamiliar as the moons of Saturn. There are a few farms and a few fishing villages around the water's edge, but by and large it lies there just like God made it, with deer and rabbit and bear and fox and many other wild animals roaming in perfect freedom their entire lives long.

Fairly near the sound lies a huge freshwater lake, somewhat larger than twice the size of Roanoke Island. It has become familiar to many hunters and fishermen. Every fall and winter literally thousands and thousands of wild geese, ducks, swans, and other migratory birds congregate on and around this beautiful lake. The lake and other nearby waters abound in fish, and the sound yields oysters and crabs and other shellfish. It is indeed a sportsman's paradise.

This was once the hunting ground of the Indian tribe known as the Mattamuskeet, a subtribe of the Algonquians and a people known for their beauty, intelligence, and bravery. When the white man first came into contact with them, the Mattamuskeet treated him with kindness and generosity. Only when they found that the whites were out to take their hunting grounds, not share them, did they turn hostile.

In the reign of King Coree the Great, long before the first white man came, the Mattamuskeets were a proud and happy people. King Coree ruled with a wise and just hand. His son, Prince Pamlico, who would inherit the position of king, was an equally wise and good man as well as a mighty hunter and fisherman. He was beloved and admired by the whole tribe, and especially by Wacheeta, the beautiful and courageous Indian maiden to whom the young prince was betrothed.

Fish and game were plentiful and close at hand, and the crops of the Indians did well in the gentle climate. The people were contented and at peace. There was no thought of saving up supplies of food against the possibility of poorer times. The hunters and fishermen took only enough to supply the immediate needs of the tribe, and the communal garden was just large enough to furnish daily fresh vegetables for the common need. It was indeed a happy land, a happy time.

Then there came a great drought over the entire country of the Mattamuskeet. For many moons it did not rain at all, and the little fields of maize were yellow and parched and produced no grain. The streams were nearly dry and were without fish of any kind. Even the weirs, the complicated fish traps the Indians built in the mighty sounds, failed to catch any fish, and the situation began to grow desperate. The wild animals of the woods and forests migrated to other places in search of food and water. Day after day the hunting parties came back empty-handed.

Actual famine and starvation now threatened the tribe as many of the children grew sickly and several of the older warriors died. The medicine men did all they knew to do, but to no avail. Every day the sun rose in a cloudless sky, and the earth and its usually green and verdant forests became more dried out and parched.

It was obvious to the Mattamuskeet that they had unwittingly done some terrible thing which had offended the Great Spirit and that they were being punished until they made the proper restitution.

King Coree called a meeting of all the subchiefs and heads of families. With the advice and counsel of the medicine men, they discussed for days this great evil that had befallen them and how they could best set things aright. In the end it was decided to make a great sacrificial fire, one that would be bigger and costlier than any ever used in the history of the tribe. They would see whether this extraordinary effort would appease the Great Spirit. They knew that fire came from the Great Spirit and that conflagrations made in his honor should please him as they had done in the past. It was worth trying.

In the middle of the village they built a huge altar of cypress wood and pine, bigger and more beautiful than anyone had seen before. Upon the altar they heaped most of the maize they had left, as well as openauk roots, dried tobacco leaves, which they called *uppowoc*, acorns, dried yaupon leaves, and other articles of daily use. The medicine men then threw upon the altar various roots, healing preparations made of bird claws and deer hoofs, dried resin from the pine trees, and many chinquapins. Over all this they piled sassafras and myrtle and juniper wood to give forth sweet odors.

Then huge lightwood knots were carefully inserted under the whole pile, and Coree the Great, himself, came forward and lit the bonfire.

The assembled tribe gathered in a great circle about the flaming altar, beating upon tom-toms and shaking their gourd rattles and shouting at the tops of their voices, so that a great noise went up into the heavens. They lacerated their bodies with the sharp edges of mussel shells, and they threw ashes and sand into the air over their heads, all the while executing intricate and wild dances, which they improvised as they danced, until they fell, exhausted and panting, around the flaming altar.

But all to no avail. The Great Spirit was displeased with their offerings and their efforts, and the fire would not continue to burn upon the altar. On the contrary, and to make matters much worse, the dried-out peat beds beneath the altar became ignited. The ceremonial fire spread through the tinder-dry leaf mold and peat and, fanned by a hot, dry wind, erupted into a great conflagration. The huge fire illuminated the entire sky that night with an angry red glow. The people almost suffocated from the smoke and stench of the burning peat. The very earth itself was ablaze and out of control, just as many of the peat beds of Ireland sometimes catch fire and burn for many feet under ground.

Day after horrible day, and on into weeks, the great fire burned and smoked. For more than thirteen moons it burned, destroying large areas of the hunting grounds but always, mercifully, being fanned away from the Indian village by a persistent wind.

When a change in that wind pattern brought a real threat to the existence of the village itself, the Mattamuskeet did not know where to turn. Another council was called, and all the people attended in great concern. Some favored migration to the country of the friendly Chowanoke, but the priests and the medicine men insisted that nothing would appease the Great Spirit now but the sacrifice of a member of their own tribe.

After much debate, the tribe agreed to obey the wishes of the medicine men, and the human victim was selected by lot. To the great dismay of all the people and to their great sorrow, the luck of the draw selected, not one of the older and less useful members of the tribe, but none other than Prince Pamlico, noblest and bravest of them all. With great dignity and with no show of fear, he accepted his selection. He went quietly to the medicine man's shelter to be prepared for the sacrificial death he was to undergo for the sake of his tribe. He began the long ceremony of shaving his head except for a topknot, of greasing his temples and neck with bear fat treated with a scarlet dye from roots, and finally of swallowing the various potions and charms prepared for him by the medicine man. The sacrifice was to be made with all deliberate speed.

As the tribe waited in grief-stricken silence for the reappearance of the sacrificial victim, there appeared before them the beautiful Wacheeta, the betrothed of the young Prince Pamlico.

It was almost unheard of for a woman to address a convocation of the people and the chiefs but, unafraid and with great earnestness, she pleaded for a brief delay in the execution of her beloved so that she might appeal to the Great Spirit in her own way.

"Before you do this thing," she said, "let me first build my own altar and invoke the mercy of our God upon us. Prince Pamlico has done nothing wrong. Perhaps the Great Spirit will not insist upon his life as the price for divine favor. At least let me try before you do the act that will make me for life a woman without a mate." The people began to murmur in sympathy with her and to cast pleading glances in the direction of the King. "So be it," he decreed. "Build your fire upon your own altar, but do not be too long about it. Even now the fire threatens the lives of all in our village."

Going back to her father's shelter, Wacheeta removed all her clothing and all the ornaments from around her neck and from her hair. Dying her face a bright crimson as a further sign of humility, she walked stark naked to the edge of the fire and picked up the unburned end of a large, blazing pine knot. Holding this aloft like a flaming banner, she walked proudly down to the edge of the waters of the broad sound and stepped into a dugout canoe made from a single juniper log.

Propping the blazing pine in the bow, she took the paddle lying in the canoe and with several strong strokes propelled the little craft to a small island just offshore where she had often played as a child. It was here, too, that she and the noble Prince Pamlico had often gone to be alone and dream their dreams, as all young folk in love have been wont to do since the beginning of time.

As the dugout gently grounded on the shelving beach of the little island, Wacheeta sprang ashore and, after dragging her canoe up on the beach, took the blazing torch and proceeded to the interior of the little island. There she built a simple altar out of the sticks and shells that lay around the scene. Then, kneeling before the flame of the pine torch, she prayed with great earnestness and with all the love she felt for the young prince. She begged for a sign to spare his life, a signal from the Great Spirit that would make the tribe, and particularly the medicine men, relent so that she could realize her dream of a long and useful life with her beloved. She prayed with all her heart. Great tears rolled down her crimson cheeks, and her voice shook with the urgency of her pleading until, finally, she fell over and lay prostrate upon the sand, exhausted.

At that very instant a great clap of thunder was heard

in the smoke-darkened skies. And then another and yet
another, as the lightning blazed brilliantly and seemed to
light up the whole of creation.

This was followed by the most torrential downpour of
rain anyone had ever seen, even in the great autumn
storms. It rained and it rained. It rained so hard that it was
impossible to see more than a few feet in front of your
eyes. It rained so that Wacheeta was afraid to try to paddle back to the mainland to find out what had happened to
her lover. She was afraid her little dugout canoe would be
filled with water and swamped by the force of the rain.

What happened back in the village was that the tribe,
believing that Wacheeta had appeased the Great Spirit,
insisted that Prince Pamlico be freed immediately and restored to his father. A great celebration began, which
lasted, despite the continuing downpour, for several days.
Prince Pamlico, as soon as he could tear himself free from
the grasp of rejoicing friends, ran down to the shore and
swam out to the little island, where he found his Wacheeta
safe and sound and crying softly in her relief.

The rain finally stopped, but not before it had completely filled the burnt-out cavities in the earth and there
was born a beautiful, sparkling lake in their stead. The
Great Spirit filled the lake with all kinds of fish and wild
fowl. The swans and the ducks and the geese came and
swam and sported about upon its bosom. Sparkling springs
fed the lake with fresh water and kept it filled to the brim.

The fields, of course, were rejuvenated by the blessed
rain, and the countryside roundabout was replenished
with game of all kinds. The deer came back, as did the

rabbits and the bear and all the other animals that had been there in such abundance before. Saved by the blessing of the rain, the entire area became green, productive, and lush once again.

And so Lake Mattamuskeet remains to this day; a limpid lake surrounded by a smiling land of beauty and plenty. So may it ever be.

14

The Fountain of Mercy

HE YEAR 1717 HAD BEEN a bad one so far for Alan and Flora McInnes. In Charleston, South Carolina, they had watched as an epidemic killed their daughter and son-in-law, Ann and James Scott, as well as scores of their friends. Their twelve-year-old grandson, Alan Scott, had come to live with them after the double funeral, and although his presence in the home had made things brighter, the McInneses desperately wanted a change of scene in a new city in this new land.

They were especially concerned about young Alan, who seemed unable to shake his mood of depression. The lad had loved both his parents, but he had been especially close to his mother, and he seemed unable to accept her loss.

And so it was that they took passage on board the brig *Sarah* on a hot and humid day in August. They wanted to visit friends in Jamestown and to try to forget the sadness of the spring and summer.

Portents of bad weather were plentiful. The air was stiflingly hot, even for August. The cloud formations, as they scudded across the sky, resembled mares' tails, portending violent winds and heavy seas. Timid souls might have been afraid to set sail under such conditions, but after all, the trip was to be a relatively short one, and the captain was able and experienced.

There was some concern, too, about the possibility of encountering pirates, but the Royal Navy was doing an increasingly efficient job of capturing the brigands, and the *Sarah* was an exceptionally fast and able boat. All in all, the risks seemed minimal.

The first two days out of Charleston saw the little ship making good progress. A following wind of almost gale force sent her swooping along "with a bone in her teeth," and although the wind continued to freshen, the captain decided against putting in at Ocracoke Inlet but continued instead on and around the point of Hatteras.

Near midnight of the second day, the seriousness of his error in judgment became apparent. The wind continued to strengthen, and the seas increased to an alarming height, becoming disorganized and unpredictable. It became necessary to strike all sail and heave the boat to. A sea anchor, or drogue, was secured by a stout line to the bowsprit of the boat and was tossed overboard in an effort to keep her head into the wind. This device eased her for a short while, but the gale continued to grow stronger and the wave motion more awesome and confused. It soon became apparent that the little ship was doomed.

The order was given to abandon ship, and the small family was herded into the longboat, which swung on davits alongside the leeward rail of the ship. No sooner had the three passengers been placed in the boat than a huge wave broke clear across the *Sarah*'s decks, smashing the davits that supported the longboat and wrenching it away from the mother ship. With a long shudder, the *Sarah* then rolled over in the maelstrom and sank beneath the wild sea. Not even the sailors who had stood by the davits were saved. Not a cry for help, not a scream of terror, was heard as the *Sarah* and all her crew went to the bottom, one more victim of this "Graveyard of the Atlantic."

How that longboat survived the sinking of the *Sarah* is known only to God. All that long night the little craft was slapped and wrenched and tossed about, while the family of three lay, in shock from sheer terror, in the bottom of the boat. There was no use to bail the water out of the longboat. Waves were continually breaking over and into it. Nor was there any need even to try to sit upright. The wild spinning and lurching motions of the boat could easily have thrown them out if they had tried that. Besides, it was easier to breathe if they could take advantage of the little lee provided by the sides of the boat. The sheer pressure of that mighty wind was awesome. They could not face into it and breathe.

Partially filled with sea water and moving sluggishly as it rode low in the water, the longboat survived the night of horror. It greeted the dawn still upright and still harboring the three exhausted survivors. The next day the winds began to abate, and soon thereafter the waves, although huge in size, became rounded, rolling hills of water rather than menacing breakers, and the small craft rode more easily. By the fourth day after the sinking, the sea had subsided.

It was hot.

The sun rose each day in a cloudless sky and beat unmercifully upon the surface of the sea, which soon calmed down to the point that it was a flat, glassy plain of water as far as the eye could reach. In complete contrast to the storm, there was now not even a breath of breeze.

The McInneses found a little relief in soaking their garments in sea water and then holding them to their feverish bodies. Little Alan Scott soon learned the trick of going over the side and hanging to the gunwale of the boat as he immersed his body up to his chin in the ocean. Although they were deathly afraid of sharks, the McInneses did not deny him this relief, and no harm ever seemed to come of it.

The survivors could not remember the exact passage of time after that. They knew only that it was unbearably hot and that there was no water and nothing to eat, and they were all very sure that they were going to die in that open boat. Only their strong belief in God kept them from joining hands and jumping overboard to put an end to their misery. It is certain that each of them was delirious at one time or another. It is also certain that each of them in his own way prayed, as earnestly and as fervently as he knew how, for the mercy of Almighty God either to deliver them from their torture or to let them die and thus end their suffering.

It could not have been many nights later that Alan McInnes awoke from a fitful slumber and looked out on the calm surface of the sea lit up with the radiance of the full moon. It was a scene that was almost unreal in its beauty and serenity.

As he looked around him, McInnes gave a start of disbelief. There, not one hundred yards away, appeared the figure of a young woman, who looked as though she were actually standing on the surface of the water. She looked almost exactly like his deceased daughter Ann. Then it seemed that the apparition spoke. And it spoke with the voice of his Ann.

"Father," it cried, "come to me. Come to the fountain of mercy, Father. You have prayed for God's mercy; now accept it. Come to me and drink of His fountain of mercy. Come and drink and cool your parched and burning throat. Come to me, Father. Come and drink."

Seizing the blade of a broken oar that lay in the boat, Alan McInnes began to paddle with all his might to reach this strange and inviting apparition. His progress was exasperatingly slow and clumsy. First the boat would swing to one side under his efforts, and then he would overcorrect and the bow would swing to the other side.

Finally, however, by dint of much frenzied labor, he managed to propel the little boat the distance he estimated the ghostly figure had been away from him. He looked up from his labors only to find that the figure had disappeared! The voice continued, however, seeming to come from all around him now. "Drink, Father, drink. Fountain of mercy. Drink, Father, drink and be saved."

With a cry of despair, the old man threw the oar blade

down in the boat and, sinking onto one of the seats, burst into tears of frustration and anguish. It had seemed so real, and now it had gone. Drink and be saved, indeed! There was nothing to drink. There was not any water at all. No water—except sea water. Now, McInnes had been told many times that to drink sea water would mean delirium and ultimate death, that it would not quench thirst but only intensify it. Nevertheless, the memory of that voice kept beating and repeating in his ears, "Drink, Father, drink and be saved." With a sigh of desperation, McInnes knelt on the seat, leaned far out over the side of the boat, submerged his entire face and head under the surface, and drank a great gulp of water.

The water of the sea was fresh! Just as fresh and sweet as mountain spring water and as grateful to his parched throat and stomach.

Awaking his wife and grandson, McInnes told them of the ghostly figure and of the fresh sea water. At first they did not believe him, but finally, after watching him drink great draughts of the water, they tasted it and then drank copiously until they were so full of the fresh water that they felt waterlogged. Crying with joy, they joined hands and knelt in the bottom of that sturdy boat and thanked their God. They did not seek to understand this miracle. They only accepted it and the merciful gift of life it brought them.

Two days later they were sighted and picked up by a passing ship, still more dead than alive, but saved by the Fountain of Mercy. The ship's captain, upon hearing their tale, sent his own longboat to fetch a barrel of the water so that he could take it to port as proof of their story. Yes, he said, he had heard of such pools of fresh water in the middle of the sea, but he had never seen one in all his life and had not expected to see one.

The ship proceeded on its way and landed the little family, now much improved in health and strength, at the town of Ocracoke, where they rested and recuperated for several weeks before continuing on their journey to Jamestown.

Now, it is quite understandable that some skeptics may doubt this story, but it is told as a true one by some of the people of our Outer Banks. They sincerely believe with simple but profound faith that prayers were answered on this occasion and that the McInneses were saved by a genuine miracle.

And who can say that they were not?

Certainly not the scientists who have now discovered that there are not one but several such freshwater areas in the ocean off our coast. They now know, these scientists, that great underground rivers of fresh water sometimes surface upon the ocean bottom with such great force and volume that a genuine fountain of pure, fresh water is intruded into the ocean, pouring undiluted from the bottom of the sea to the surface of the ocean itself. Thus is created a "Fountain of Mercy" for those who are in desperate need of the life-sustaining waters and who happen to go (or are sent) to that particular spot on the surface of the sea where this phenomenon is occurring. Some of these underground rivers or streams, called "aquifers" by the geologists, actually originate in the mountains of this state, and some come to the "surface" on the bottom of our sounds. Such is the giant Castle Hayne Aquifer, which surfaces in Pamlico Sound.

The ghostly apparition?

Maybe not entirely the hallucination of a man about to die of thirst in an open boat. When that cold mountain river water comes into violent, upsurging collision with the warm waters of and around the Gulf Stream, is it not natural to expect some sort of mist or vapor to result? Fishermen know the dense fogs and mists that can result when bodies of water of differing temperatures come into sudden conflict.

At any rate, the little family was saved from an agonizing death on the flat surface of a glassy, blue sea. They have provided the citizens of the Outer Banks—and through them have provided us—with another of the wonderful stories that the Bankers tell and believe as the very truth. They see the Fountain of Mercy as just another indication and proof that prayer, real sincere and earnest prayer, can and does bring about miracles.

This they believe. This I believe with them.

15

The Queen of the Sounds

NOT ALL THE GHOSTS which (or who) inhabit North Carolina's Outer Banks are ancient. Some, including the ghost in this story, are less than a hundred years old. Like the famous ghost ships and ghost crabs, many ghosts cannot claim ever to have existed in human form, but their spectral carryings-on continue to this very day to have a profound effect on humans.

For the beginnings of our story we must go back to those days after the War Between the States. Roanoke Island had been captured by General Ambrose Burnside, the Union officer whose name and coiffure created a new word in the American language. The General had left a holding force on the island when he moved on to other theatres of action. Among those occupying troops was a roistering young corporal named Pierre "Frenchy" Godette, who was devoted to whiskey, gambling, and general cain-raising, in that order.

Frenchy Godette had himself a ball during the entire time he was stationed on Roanoke Island. The duty was extremely light, and even in those days a copious supply of excellent corn whiskey was available at a cheap price from the nearby mainland. Most of Frenchy's comrades-in-arms were congenial, and their predilections were not unlike those of the Corporal himself.

Corporal Godette fell in love with the region. The climate was salubrious, the people were honest and forth-right, and nature had provided an abundance of food, such as wild game and fish, which could be had for the expenditure of very little effort.

It is no wonder, then, that Godette determined to make coastal Carolina and the Outer Banks in particular his permanent home. By pulling some strings and by seeing the right people, he got himself appointed as a commissioner when he mustered out of the army, and thus he was able to move into the Reconstruction Era with a cushy federal job.

Although life continued to be an almost unbroken spree for him, Frenchy did attend to his new job passably well, and he did stay out of trouble. The cost of living on Roanoke Island was very reasonable at that time, and he was able to put by a sizable sum of money before Congress finally abolished his job. This put him, for the first time in his forty years, in the position of having to look for a means of making a living.

The Southland was just beginning to revive then, with industry and commerce picking up over the entire region. Frenchy Godette became aware of this trend for the better, and he was determined to ride the crest of the wave of increasing prosperity. One of the most serious shortcomings of the entire region, as Frenchy saw it, was the almost total lack of commercial entertainment. The people needed somewhere to go, something to do to provide themselves with a little pleasure. Godette intended to provide a place where the people could enjoy his type of good time to any degree they could afford.

Investing almost his entire savings, the former corporal privately commissioned the building of a showboat! Skilled boatbuilding services were still relatively cheap, and the very finest cypress and juniper timbers were readily available. The broad-beamed, shallow-drafted stern-wheeler was almost a year in the building.

When finally completed, she was, indeed, a thing of beauty and convenience. She had three decks, one above the other. On the first or main deck, there was a tremendous ballroom amidships, which was to double as a theatre when dancing was not in progress. A large bar or saloon was fitted with leather upholstered seats all around the sides. In the center of the room, tables with matching chairs offered a wide choice of gambling games, almost any card game at all, and for any stakes the plunger wished to risk. On the upper decks were banistered promenades, which opened into private rooms that could be used for any number of pursuits. The draperies and the bar fittings were all imported from Paris and added an extra touch of luxury to the already resplendent vessel.

The boat was powered by a tremendous steam engine, the huge boiler taking up almost the entire hold beneath the ballroom. A broad rear deck near the paddle wheel gave ample space for storing the wood fuel she burned.

But the crowning touch, the thing that really set the big craft apart and made her an object of admiration and awe throughout all the coastal regions of northeastern North Carolina, was that marvelous, brand-new invention, the huge player piano! No one in the whole area had ever even heard of a player pianoforte, much less seen or heard one. This was the largest and the loudest player piano available, and it had been manufactured under the direct supervision of the inventor himself.

Every available roll of music was purchased and put on board, and there was one member of the crew whose sole duty it was to attend to the marvel, to operate it as he had been especially trained to do, and to change the rolls to suit the tastes of his audience. When turned up full blast, this musical phenomenon could be heard for several miles across the quiet waters of the coastal sounds.

The floating palace was christened the *Queen of the Sounds*, and whether she was named for the waters over which she operated or for the melodious noises that emanated from her ballroom on moonlit nights, the name was entirely appropriate.

For two years she operated up and down the broad sounds of North Carolina, stopping for days at a time in such places as Edenton and Plymouth and Elizabeth City and Manteo and Currituck. From time to time troupes of traveling players were engaged in Norfolk or Philadelphia to stay on board and perform the popular plays of the era for the entranced folk of the tidewater towns where the *Queen* made her scheduled stops.

Saloon "hostesses" were a regular part of the scene, furnishing feminine companionship to the drinkers at the bar or to the gamblers at the nearby tables. When the *Queen of the Sounds* tied up at the wharf of a coastal town, most of the work in that town would likely cease, and a spirit of carnival would prevail over the entire community until she cast off her lines and departed for the next stop. She was, indeed, many things to many people, and she brightened the lives of many of the coastal residents. Her people were expected to observe rather strict discipline, and very seldom did any trouble occur ashore.

The *Queen* traveled continuously during the spring, summer, and autumn. She would lay up for the winter season to repaint and refurbish for the next year. Frenchy Godette was making money hand over fist and was becoming quite a wealthy man.

All might have gone quite well with Godette, and he would probably have lived what he considered to be a luxurious life (as long as his liver held out), if he had not begun to consort with a young woman who was suspected of being a witch.

Now, Frenchy was bored and spoiled and blasé. He was looking for excitement and novelty, so the lady in question had an immediate fascination for him. It was true, he found out, that she did practice black magic and that she did claim to be in touch with the Devil. She taught Frenchy several spells and incantations, and she led him ever deeper and deeper into a belief in the considerable powers of His Satanic Majesty. Thus the Devil gained a willing courtier.

All that second winter, when the *Queen of the Sounds* was laid up for repairs and redecorating, Frenchy saw the lady several times a week and became more and more fascinated with her claims of demoniac power. His drinking increased along with his obsession, until he finally became like a man possessed.

Finally, when spring came around and it was time for the *Queen* to begin her regular rounds of the coastland towns, Godette delayed and found excuses not to set out. He became preoccupied with the notion that he must head a coven of witches and warlocks and that he must, himself, summon the Devil to be his partner.

After much delay, he finally sailed the *Queen* down the sound and anchored her off the town of Wanchese, in the waters between Roanoke and Bodie islands. The *Queen* was without her usual complement of actors and actresses, but the faithful crew was on board and the bartenders were on hand, as were the saloon hostesses and ship's gamblers. A few people had looked forward to the arrival of the *Queen* with such anticipation that they went out in small boats to her unusual location rather than wait for her to dock at the town itself. She had already become a tradition. These few visitors found that she was still the same magnificent craft, all right, but the atmosphere was just not the same. Something was obviously wrong.

Finally, Frenchy let it be known that he was going to convene a coven of witches and warlocks and that he, Frenchy, was actually going to summon the Devil himself to come on board the *Queen*. Perhaps the worst of all, he proposed to do this on the very next Sunday night.

Delegations of citizens from Wanchese and Manteo took boats out to the *Queen* and implored Godette not to undertake any such scandalous and sacrilegious thing. They warned him of dire consequences if he should even try, but he was adamant. Sadly shaking their heads, the townspeople returned to their homes fully convinced that the man they had known and even sometimes despised had now become worthy of their pity. They were sure that whiskey had at last driven him insane. And who is to say that it had not?

Along about dusk on that Sunday night the tension began to build. No customers came aboard. The *Queen* was usually closed on Sunday nights anyway, and the islanders wanted no part of such profane and provocative goings on as they had heard were to take place.

The many watchers on the nearby shore could see by the brilliant illumination of the *Queen*'s lights the shadowy figure of her owner and captain standing on the very top deck with his arms outstretched toward the sea to the east. They thought they heard a stentorian call from that lonely figure, which began, "Come, Lord Satan, and receive the homage of your devoted servants—" when, all of a sudden, the voice was blotted out by the tremendous sound of the player pianoforte blaring out a dance hall tune.

Nobody is sure exactly what happened after that. The player piano continued to play at top volume unceasingly until nearly midnight. Various forms and shapes were seen in mysterious movement about the decks of the *Queen*, and eerie lights and beacons flashed on and off without apparent cause or pattern. Off to the northwest, an ominous black cloud began to roll toward the scene, but the waters of the sound were as calm as a lake. Not even a ripple from a breaking fish disturbed that brooding, stifling calm.

Then, right on the stroke of midnight, the listeners on the shore heard a high-pitched, piercing scream, as though from a soul in mortal terror. So loud and so piercing was this scream that it could be heard distinctly even above the tremendous volume of the player piano.

Even as that scream of terror echoed toward the shore, there occurred the most violent and awful explosion in the memory of those onlookers. The *Queen* seemed to lift bodily out of the water amid a tremendous roar and a flash of blinding light. The beautiful vessel simply disintegrated into a million flaming pieces of wreckage, which fell, hissing, back into the calm waters.

Nobody on board survived to tell what had happened. In the heroic tradition of their forefathers, the Wanchese men immediately rowed out to the scene of the disaster in search of survivors, but they could not find so much as one body. A very strong smell of sulphur permeated the whole area, but there was never a sign of life. Thus died the *Queen* and all her crew, as well as her demented captain.

Now, many people have various explanations of this. Some say that it was simply the tremendous explosion of that huge boiler, neglected in the crew's preoccupation with superstition. It certainly could have happened that way. That was the theory held by Captain Martin Johnson, long-time captain of the vessel *Trenton*, which for so many years made weekday trips from Elizabeth City down to Nag's Head and Manteo. Cap'n Johnson used to tell this story to the kids among his passengers, much to our delight, although he never once in the hearing of this audience admitted to the existence of anything like witchcraft.

Others say that the Devil came to claim his own and that he put on a show to impress the fearful ones ashore. And that seems reasonable, too.

Still others hold firm to the belief that the Almighty himself, fed up with all that blasphemy, just wiped out the floating Gomorrah with one blow, maybe by means of a lightning bolt from an approaching northwest squall.

But the thing didn't stop there.

Many highly respectable, truthful people will swear to you in all seriousness that, if you stand near the little bridge on the causeway between Roanoke Island and Nag's Head around midnight on some hot, calm, still night in summer, you can distinctly hear the sound of that magnificent player piano grinding out its tunes. You can even see the reflection of the *Queen*'s lights on the still water.

Whatever, or whoever, is playing that ghost music on that old player piano must certainly be timeless and must have access to the music of the present century, because not only can you hear those lilting French dance hall tunes, but you can also sometimes hear such compositions as "The Old Piano Roll Blues," "When the Saints Go Marching In," and many others that had not even been composed when the *Queen of the Sounds* came to her untimely end.

Down near Coquina Beach near the Bodie Island Light-house and even over at the place that used to be known as the Duck Island Hunt Club, the tunes come in with particular clarity.

At any rate, the ghost (if it is a ghost) seems to be perfectly harmless and has occasioned a great deal of pleasant talk among coastal visitors as well as the permanent residents.

As far as is known, nobody has ever tried to approach the phenomenon by boat, so what would happen if you did is unknown. If I were you, I would not attempt to communicate any requests for tunes on the piano. Just relax and enjoy the music that is already on the program.